"You are telling me
that you are—"

"Ceci Gramont?" She flung the name at Lord Sherlay. "Yes, that is what I am telling you. I'm sorry I wed you under an assumed name, but it was not *quite* assumed."

"It . . . it is not possible."

"I fear you are angered, my Lord, but you are not quite the loser, are you?" She regarded him coldly, but at the sight of his white, still face and furious eyes, her hand inched toward her reticule. He wrested it from her, throwing it to the floor. It fell with a thud.

"Did you think to shoot me or stab me?" He seized her in his arms and bore her toward the bed.

"Let me go, let me go," she cried. "You cannot want me now!"

"On the contrary, Madame," he said between his teeth . . .

Second Chance at Love

REGENCY

LUCIA CURZON

THE CHADBOURNE LUCK

A JOVE BOOK

Requests for permission to make copies of any part
of the work should be mailed to: Permissions,
Jove Publications, Inc., 200 Madison Avenue,
New York, NY 10016

First Jove edition published June 1981

First Printing

"Second Chance at Love" and the butterfly emblem are trademarks
belonging to Jove Publications, Inc.

Printed in the United States of America

Jove books are published by Jove Publications, Inc.,
200 Madison Avenue, New York, NY 10016

— Part One —

1

CLOUDS. MISS CECI GRAMONT, moving over the tender green grass that was sprouting in Hyde Park, looked at them a little warily. Odd how quickly, the one—an elephant-shaped mass, the trunk and ears perfectly delineated until a change of wind swept them back and away—had become many, almost obliterating the blue yet making the passages between them look even bluer by contrast. It was almost as though they had been newly scrubbed and polished like the marble floor in the hall of Bella's house.

Thinking about her sister Arabella, Miss Gramont had another analogy for the clouds. When she and Mrs. Moulton had left the house on Cheyne Row that morning, there had been only a small patch of white in the sky. She had compared it to her state of mind which should have been totally springlike—she loved March, now in its lamb-guise, loved being in Chelsea, so close to London, yet there was a slight cloud on her happiness. It was not poor Mrs. Demdyke's death, though that had been painful enough, the woman having been her nurse since her birth and her constant com-

3

panion in the last six years. It was the odd feeling that
though Bella had been welcoming and full of plans for her
younger sister's brief stay in her house, she had not seemed
entirely glad to see her. With the arrival of more clouds,
Ceci was correspondingly uneasy. It was as though her
troubles were also multiplying.

"You are refining upon it too much, Miss Ceci. Such
an imagination as you have!"

She started, recognizing Nanny's voice. She had actually
glanced over her shoulder before realizing that she had
guessed how her nurse would have reacted had she been
a party to her inner confusion. No doubt, she would have
been right. There was no reason Bella should not be as
delighted to welcome her as she had insisted she was on
Ceci's arrival four days earlier. It was just that she was
very busy, appearing as Polly Peachum in a Drury Lane
revival of *The Beggar's Opera* and learning lines for *The
Castle Spectre* during the day. Ceci had seen Bella at the
theater the previous evening. She had been very proud of
her sister. Bella had made a sprightly yet ardent Polly and
Lord Madreston, who was one of Bella's admirers, had
averred that she had quite outshone their mother, whom he
had seen in the role twenty years earlier. Though Ceci's
memory of the late Sophronia Gramont was dim, and though
she had been a noted beauty, Ceci was equally positive that
Bella did outshine her. She felt a twinge of envy, wishing
that she might have resembled her sister, who was an enchanting combination of both parents, being very fair like
Mama and tall like Papa.

"I cannot imagine where you had your coloring from,
Miss Ceci."

Nanny had made this remark over and over again—as
she had glanced at Celia's dark wavy hair and eyes which,
though blue, were at least a shade deeper than those of
either Bella or George. Furthermore, at sixteen, she was
at least half a head shorter than Bella. There was a chance,
however, that this particular situation might change—

George had grown several inches after his eighteenth year. She sighed. Sometimes it seemed to her as if she could hardly wait until she was eighteen to see if she would have that spurt of growth. Meanwhile, she was barely five feet tall and at a great disadvantage in crowds, though it would have been fine for the stage, where she would have seemed, at least, an appropriate height. However, unlike her late mama and Bella, she had no talent for acting. That had been only too apparent the previous afternoon when she had prompted her sister for her part as Angela in *The Castle Spectre*. Her lackluster reading had drawn the tart comment, "It's well you've no need to earn your livelihood upon the boards—I never heard lines read with less fervor."

"But how might I put fervor in anything so silly?" Ceci had retorted and, striking an attitude, had repeated a portion of Osmond's soliloquy. " 'Mine she is, mine she shall be though Reginald's bleeding ghost flit before me, and thunder in my ear, "Hold, Hold," Peace stormy heart, here she comes.' How can a ghost bleed and if he flits—he can't thunder. He would not have enough strength."

Bella had choked back an unwilling laugh, saying sternly, "You are not to question the sense of it. You are only to cue me. And it is not silly—it is very effective on stage and I am looking forward to playing Angela."

She had been partially appeased at Ceci's assertion that she knew her sister must grace the role—but, and here the cloud floated into her mind again, the last time she had been with Bella, she had not been so edgy and elusive. In four days, she had seen her only briefly and she had not once come into her room at night to gossip, as had been her wont when she had visited her in the country. Instead, she had retired to her own chamber which was in the front of the house and a floor below, not to emerge until very late in the morning and, in spite of lying abed so long, looking tired and as if she had slept very badly.

"Dear me, I believe it will rain." Mrs. Moulton's voice roused Ceci from her thoughts. Glancing at the sky, she saw that the clouds had gone from white to a dark gray, completely blotting out the sun. "I should have brought an umbrella. The day looked so clear." Mrs. Moulton's glance at Ceci was accusing. "I'd no notion you would want to walk so far into the park."

"Far?" Ceci echoed. "We've not walked any distance at all."

"Not by *country* standards, I daresay." Mrs. Moulton's tone seemed to disparage both the country and her charge.

Ceci bristled at the insinuation, mentally decrying the fact that Bella had chosen this woman to be her chaperon. Mrs. Moulton, a thin, middle-aged actress, had, for reasons of health, retired from the theater, where she had been known for her impeccable portrayals of grandes dames. In private life her demeanor remained much the same and her air of awesome gentility was, Bella had declared, just what was needed for her sister. "I should go about with you, myself, child, had I the time, but since I do not, we are very fortunate in securing the services of Mrs. Moulton. I shall breathe easier knowing that you are in her company."

Under those circumstances, Ceci thought drearily, she dared not tell her sister that she would as lief have done without Mrs. Moulton's companionship. It behooved the girl not to take umbrage at her chaperon's lofty set-downs, not if she were to continue to enjoy the sights of London. She said, "I am sorry we came so far. I had not noticed . . . oh!" She glanced upward at a sky from which large drops of rain were now descending.

"Come," Mrs. Moulton said urgently, "we must seek a tree. We cannot possibly reach the gates." She was casting frantic eyes about her as she spoke, evidently sizing up various trees and find each of them wanting. "Ah . . ." she began. "There . . ."

"If I might be of assistance," someone said hesitantly.

Ceci, glancing around, saw a tall, slender man in a curly, brimmed beaver and wearing a fashionable many-caped coat. He was holding a large black umbrella and now he proffered it toward Mrs. Moulton.

The chaperon regarded him with some consternation, a refusal trembling on the edge of her tongue. She had been instructed not to encourage any of the young gallants Arabella Gramont feared might cast eyes on her charge, but, she thought desperately as the rain increased in intensity, surely casting an umbrella was a different matter. "That would be extremely kind of you," she said in the condescending tones she had employed when playing Lady Mary Oldboys of *Lionel and Clarissa*, a role for which she had been much praised.

"Oh, it really would." Ceci beamed up at him. "We stand to be exceptionally wet."

He smiled. "Then I pray that both of you charming ladies will possess yourself of my arms and I trust we shall do tolerably well."

Ceci did not hesitate to take his left arm and upon Mrs. Moulton's firmly grasping his right, he raised his umbrella and they set off. Notwithstanding the pelting of the rain and the muddy condition of the paths, they reached the park gates almost too quickly for Ceci, who on stealing several shy glances at their escort had formed an instant liking for him. Though she had no talent for acting, she did have some ability at sketching and she wished she had brought her pad so that she might have penciled in features which she found extremely pleasing. There was generosity and good humor reflected in his countenance. He had a broad forehead, large, well-spaced hazel-green eyes, a straight nose, and a wide firm mouth, quirked at the corners into what seemed a habitual smile. She had always admired a cleft chin and she also liked the color of his hair, which was a dark auburn and clustered at his temples in large loose ringlets. About George's height, she observed, and thought he must be much of her brother's years, which numbered twenty. By the time they had emerged from the park and were across the street, where he was obligingly hailing a hackney for them, she was full of regrets that she probably would not be seeing this helpful stranger again. Then, as the conveyance approached, Mrs. Moulton broke a short silence by saying, "You have been kind, sir. I am sure you have saved us both from catching cold."

"I am delighted to have been of service," he said courteously, his eyes lingering on Ceci's face.

Meeting his glance, Ceci suddenly blurted, "I am Miss Ceci Gramont and this is Mrs. Moulton. Might I know your name, sir?"

"Ceci, dear!" expostulated Mrs. Moulton, giving her a quelling glance.

"But of course you may know it," returned their rescuer, "I am Sherlay . . . uh . . . Armin Sherlay."

"Armin Sherlay," Ceci repeated. "It sounds French—but you do not."

"Ceci," breathed Mrs. Moulton.

"I expect it might have been French in Norman times— and the Sherlay spelled with a C at the beginning and a T at the end."

"Very likely," commented Ceci. "Our name is French, too, and Papa's ancestor, a Sieur de Gramont, also rode with William the Conqueror." A snorting and a jingling alerted her to the presence of the hackney.

"Come," Mrs. Moulton prompted. As the cabman hastily opened the door for the ladies, she bent her austere gaze on their rescuer. "I do thank you, sir. Dreadful weather. I pray it will not rain tomorrow afternoon when we go to St. Paul's."

"I cannot think but that it was a passing cloudburst," he returned, looking past her at Ceci.

"I hope it is," Ceci said. "There's so much of London I want to see."

"I, too," he responded. "Are you new to the city, too?"

"Almost . . . I was born in London, but I have been living in the country for the past eight years."

"My dear Ceci, we must be on our way. Your sister will be worried," Mrs. Moulton said, ushering her into the hackney.

"Good-bye." Ceci waved. "And you were ever so nice."

"I enjoyed our walk," he called.

"Good afternoon, sir," Mrs. Moulton said coolly.

"Armin Sherlay..." Ceci murmured as the hackney started up. "Is not that a lovely name, Mrs. Moulton?"

"The name is not unknown to me," Mrs. Moulton observed. "There was a Viscount Sherlay who was a particular friend of a friend of mine, and now that I think on it, this young man has something of the look of him. I imagine he might be his son."

"Oh, why did you not say so!" Ceci exclaimed.

"It was not my place to claim acquaintance," Mrs. Moulton said primly.

"But you believe you know his father..."

"My friend might have known his father," Mrs. Moulton contradicted, if, indeed, there is a relationship. I, however, had but a nodding acquaintance with him. I might mention that you were very bold in your own address. It was not up to you to ask his name."

"But I wanted to know it," Ceci said. "Oh, dear, I should like to see him again."

"I should not count on it," Mrs. Moulton said dampeningly. She added, "Also... though above all things I dislike dissembling, I think it were better that you did not mention this... encounter to your sister."

Ceci's wide eyes grew wider. "But why not?"

"Because I am sure that dear Arabella would not be pleased at our proffering encouragement to an unknown young gentleman."

"How did we encourage him?" Ceci demanded. "We should have been soaked to the skin had we not accepted his offer of an umbrella."

"All the same, I cannot think that your sister would approve," Mrs. Moulton said uncomfortably.

"Very well, I shall not mention it," Ceci promised. She added dreamily, "But would it not be lovely if he were to go to the theater and see Bella as Polly. Then he could come backstage and meet her and I should be in her dressing room as I was last night but . . ." She suddenly frowned. "It would not serve, would it?"

"Such a happening would be most unlikely," Mrs. Moulton said dryly.

"Actually, I am glad of that—for once he saw Bella, I should be quite cast in the shade."

"It would be better were you to put this afternoon's episode from your thoughts."

"It cannot hurt for me to think about him," Ceci murmured. "Armin Sherlay . . . such a lovely name. I do not believe I shall ever forget it—or him. Oh, I do wish I were beautiful like Bella. Then he would not have just put me into a hackney and waved good-bye. He would have begged to accompany me back to my dwelling and . . ."

"He would have done nothing of the sort," Mrs. Moulton said sternly. "No gentleman of breeding would act in so untoward a manner with a genteel female. Surely you must know that."

Again Ceci caught that disparaging note in her companion's voice. Twin sparks shone in her eyes. "I do know it, Mrs. Moulton. I am not so green as all that. It is just that . . . I should so like to see him again."

"Well, if you do not," Mrs. Moulton commented unsympathetically, "you will no doubt meet many other young gentlemen equally personable."

"Oh, no," Ceci said positively, "I am sure I never, never shall." Catching an odd look in the chaperon's eye, she tried to define the expression. It had seemed almost calculating, she thought, and instinctively did not like it. She braced herself for one more of that lady's acid remarks but none was forthcoming. She merely turned away and stared out the window. Feeling uncomfortable, Ceci wished once more that Bella had not chosen this woman to accompany her—she did not know quite why, but she was sure Nanny would never have approved of her. Then her thoughts were deflected by the view of another black umbrella, which sight brought back the smiling face of their rescuer. With a little pang that again escaped total definition, she mentally relived every moment of that walk across the park, and as she did, a line that the poet Marlowe had attributed to Leander arose in her mind, "Whoever loved, who loved not at first sight?" A warm flush mounted her cheeks. "But it is impossible!" she muttered.

"I beg your pardon?" Mrs. Moulton's gaze was again directed toward her charge. "What did you say?"

Ceci knew that her blush had deepened and that knowledge only served to heighten the glow. "N-Nothing," she replied nervously. "I . . . I was only thinking out loud."

"That's a habit you'll need to overcome—else folk'll think you daft."

Ceci's long dark lashes veiled her resentful stare. Yet, thinking on it, she wondered herself if she had not turned slightly daft. One could not fall in love with a complete stranger in the space of time it took to negotiate a relatively small stretch of ground. Of course . . . in *Romeo and Juliet*, but that was a play and, as Bella was wont to say and not always happily, real life was seldom like that imagined by the dramatists.

"Oh, I wish it were," Ceci murmured under her breath, "for then I should surely see him again . . . and in the second act."

"It is so high!" Ceci standing before the colonnaded portico of St. Paul's Cathedral, sketchpad in hand, gazed upward at the great dome flanked by twin towers and set on Corinthian columns similar to those at the entrance and, on a higher level, supported the sculptured pediment. She extracted a charcoal stick from her reticule. "I think I should like to draw a bit of it."

"Why do we not go into the building, first?" Mrs. Moulton suggested.

"Shall we?" she asked doubtfully. "It's bound to be chilly and it is so pleasant here in the sunshine."

"If you would not mind, I have a rock in my slipper and I should like to sit down and take it out."

"Oh, then, of course we must go in," Ceci said instantly. "I hope it does not hurt you."

"No, no." For some reason, Mrs. Moulton flushed. "It is only uncomfortable."

As she had anticipated, the vast interior of the cathedral was not only cold but damp. She felt its chill through her woolen gown and even through her padded pelisse. However, the paintings and sculptures were enough to make her forget her immediate discomfort. "Oh," she breathed. "I am glad we are here."

"Yes, I thought it well that you should see the work of Sir Christopher Wren, Ceci, as well as that of Grinling Gibbons, who was one of the sculptors who contributed his art to this magnificent edifice. Gibbons, as you know, also sculpted that fine statue of King Charles II which stands in front of the Royal Hospital."

"In-indeed." Ceci spoke in a low voice, hoping devoutly that Mrs. Moulton would not see her twitching lips as she struggled to button down her smile and swallow her laughter. Though her chaperon was probably unaware of it, her trained voice had been unnaturally loud, booming through the stillness and arousing a host of echoes in the dim distances of that mighty interior. Several people had turned from contemplation of the masterworks that lined the walls to stare at her. Finally she was able to stifle her laughter and she said, "Might you point out the work of Mr. Gibbons?"

"Perhaps you may find it for yourself, my dear," Mrs. Moulton instructed in a somewhat lower register. "I must see to this rock, but I pray that you will remain within a short distance of the chairs that I may see where you are."

"Oh, I shall," Ceci assured her, moving hastily away, thankful at this unexpected if momentary release from Mrs. Moulton's oppressive company. Yet, as she looked about her, she was confused. There was so much to see! Conversely, she almost wished that Mrs. Moulton had remained with her to explain it. Frowning a little, she moved along a side aisle, examining the paintings. Then she heard a step behind her.

"I may not offer you an umbrella, Miss Gramont, but I might answer the question you asked about Grinling Gibbons. He is known to have executed the choir stalls."

Startled, she whirled about. "Mr. Sherlay!" she breathed, looking up at features she had pictured through much of the previous afternoon and which had still been in her mind when she had awakened that morning. "Oh, how lovely!" she cried joyfully and then blushed. "I . . . mean . . ."

His laughter, equally joyful, broke across the beginning of what promised to be an extremely garbled disclaimer. "Well met, Miss Gramont. Shall I show you Grinling Gibbons' choir stalls?"

"Yes, indeed, I should very much like to view them. But . . ." She looked toward the chairs and was momentarily taken aback. "She is not there!" she exclaimed.

"Who?" he inquired.

"Mrs. Moulton. She was fixing her shoe. She had a rock in it. She said I was not to stray from her sight."

"She cannot chide you for going to seek the work of Gibbons since she desired especially that you look at it."

"Oh, you heard her!" Ceci bit down a giggle.

"I am sure that she was heard in heaven. Yet, I can only be pleased that she speaks with such clarity—for I owe my presence here to those ringing tones."

"You mean because you heard her speak and recognized her voice from yesterday?" Cecil asked. Then, before he could answer, she added amazedly, "It is certainly the greatest coincidence that you happened to be in the cathedral at the same time as we."

"No, it was no coincidence." He smiled. "I heard her say yesterday that you were coming to St. Paul's this afternoon. I was on the point of believing you must have changed your mind when I heard her dulcet shout."

Ceci stared up at him in consternation. "You are saying that you came here *especially* to meet us?"

"No, I am saying that I came here especially to meet *you*. I pray you'll not think me too bold."

"Oh, I do not. I was so praying that I might see you again." Her cheeks burned. "I mean . . ."

"I hope that you mean exactly what you have just said. Please do not tell me that you did not mean it," he begged.

"I shan't tell you that—because it would not be true, but I am quite certain I never should have said so." She looked down quickly.

"No, if you were to abide by all the silly rules of conduct that we, who are young, are forced to observe, you should never have said it—but I wish to tell you that I am equally glad to see you and should have been most miserable had you not arrived. I shall further explain that I have been here since before noon, anxiously pacing the length and breadth of this cathedral, wondering when and if you would arrive. So we are both culprits."

"Oh." Impulsively Ceci put out her hand and then would quickly have taken it back had he not caught it in his warm grasp. At his touch, she was conscious of a series of pulses at odd places all over her body.

"Come," he said breathlessly. "I have promised to show you the choir stalls. Should you like to see them? They are wonderfully carved."

"Oh, yes." Ceci nodded. "I expect I should." She glanced at the sea of chairs. "I cannot think what has happened to Mrs. Moulton. It's very puzzling."

"Does it matter?"

"No, I am glad not to find her. I . . . I am not much in sympathy with her, though again I expect I should not say so."

"You should always say what you mean and it is quite understandable. She is a bit of a dragon."

"Oh, she is," Ceci agreed.

"But," he said, smiling, "she is a good dragon to have flown away and left us in peace. Shall we be off before she wings back breathing fire?"

"Oh, yes," she responded with alacrity.

Releasing her hand, he took her arm, guiding her along the aisle.

"There is a work by Jonathan Maine," he said, indicating a sculpture.

"It is lovely," Ceci said automatically, her eyes flicking over it and taking in none of it. It was hard to direct her thoughts into any coherent pattern. It was equally difficult for her to obtain a clear aspect of what she was seeing. Fluted columns, vaulted roof, the paintings, the statuary, all seemed to meld into one mass, and that a background for the man who strode beside her. His touch, his nearness was the only reality of which she was aware. She had the odd feeling that rather than merely walking with him, she was flying she knew not whither.

"And this"—his voice was threaded with laughter—"is Nicholas Stone's famed statue of John Donne:"

"Of John Donne, yes." Ceci murmured, raising bedazzled eyes.

"Can you believe that he posed for it *before* his death?" he demanded.

"Before . . ." At that moment, her gaze became focused and she found herself confronting the likeness of the poet, eyes shut, spare body wrapped in a winding sheet and standing on a funerary urn. "Ohhhhhh . . ." She shuddered. "You say he was *alive* when this was done?"

"Very much so, though he was ill and thought he'd not

long to live, which was true."

"But why should he anticipate death in so horrid a manner?"

"A melancholy disposition and a somewhat disordered mind. Last year at Cambridge, I read Izaak Walton's *Life of Donne*. He had a hard unhappy life. His wife, whom he must have idolized, had been dead some fourteen years and I think he was anxious to join her."

"Poor man," Ceci murmured. "Yet, though I like his poetry, I remember he seemed to think slightingly of females."

Her companion's eyes gleamed and then closing them, he recited:

> "Yet send me back my heart and eyes,
> That I may know and see thy lies,
> And may laugh and joy, when thou
> > Art in anguish
> > And dost languish
> > > For someone
> > > That will none
> Or prove as false as thou art now."

"Oh, you do say it beautifully . . . and you've conned it well."

"I've heard it often," he explained. "I've a friend who often quotes Donne to me. His heart was early blighted . . . in common with the poet, perhaps."

"Yet, John Donne must have loved his wife since he was so anxious to join her."

"I think he did—but poets are fond of spurious pain. There was one I knew at the university—a youth named Byron, who was forever writing about unrequited love and death. There was merit to his work, but from talking to him, I found his suffering to be little felt. It is likely this is true of many who have versified about love."

"It ought to rouse happier sentiments," she contended.

"It soon will . . . for I shall pen one such."

"Oh, do you write poetry?" she demanded excitedly.

"I've not had an inclination for it until now, but I feel a muse has lit upon my shoulder and she tells me you've remarkable eyes to which a sonnet must be dedicated."

"You are funning me!" she accused.

"I am not."

Meeting his gaze, the pulses in her body seemed to mass and congregate in her throat. "My . . . eyes are no more than . . . well, just eyes." She tried to speak lightly but was not sure she had been successful.

"You are no judge of them."

"They are merely blue while yours are green and gold and brown all at the same time."

"There!" He laughed. "I said you were no judge of eyes. Mine are muddy hazel, while yours are no ordinary blue but the color of a deep woodland pool at twilight, and I am sure that no one has ever possessed such extraordinarily long lashes!"

"You ought to see . . ." She paused. She had been on the point of mentioning Bella, but to mention her sister was to rouse his interest, and if he were to even glimpse her—but he must not, not yet. She did not want him to be aware of Bella's existence!

"What must I see?" he prompted.

"I . . . I forgot what I was about to say," she stammered, feeling remarkably foolish. "I think we must both see those choir stalls."

"I cannot believe that that is what you meant to tell me, O, mysterious maiden."

"Mysterious maiden!" She dimpled. "I am not in the least mysterious."

"But you are. Other than your name and the fact that Norman blood flows blue in your veins—I know nothing about you."

"Nor I about you," she countered, "save that you are called Armin Sherlay—which is such a beautiful name. Do you live in London?"

"I have for the last three months, since I came down from Cambridge."

"In the middle of the term?"

"I decided not to finish."

"But why?"

He shrugged. "I'd been there three years and found it passing dull at the last. Since I'm not to be a solicitor or a diplomat or a pedagogue, I believe I am tolerably well educated. If I am not, I can resume my studies in my own library, which, thanks to the efforts of my uncle, is exceedingly well stocked."

"What will you do, then?"

"I'd thought to kick up my heels a bit . . . then retire to pasture at Briarton Abbey."

"Briarton Abbey? Deeded to your family by Henry VIII?"

"Yes . . . have you heard of it, then?"

"No, but I thought all abbeys were annexed during that period."

"That is true. It belonged to the Benedictines. I'm afraid my ancestor helped drive the monks away. He was well cursed for his efforts."

"Cursed?" She shivered slightly. "How?"

"Oh, with various miseries which came to naught." He shrugged. "I do not believe curses can wreak harm unless those who have suffered them give credence to the threats." He smiled. "But enough. It seems I have told you a good deal about myself and yet I know nothing about you."

"There's precious little to know."

"You're yet determined upon being mysterious, I see." He laughed.

"I am not in the least mysterious," she contradicted.

"Unless you tell me more about yourself, I shan't believe that. Start with giving me your age, which I judge to be about seventeen or possibly less."

It was on the tip of her tongue to tell him that she was but a fortnight past her sixteenth birthday, but it was possible he might believe her far too young. "I am seventeen and four months," she said.

"Then I guessed right. Where do you live?"

"In the Village of Chelsea."

"Ah, Chelsea. I am not yet familiar with London's environs. You've lived there long?"

She shook her head. "Under a week. As I have told you, I've been in the country with my nurse, who looked after me when my parents died. I shall soon be returning to the country when I go to join my brother in Northumberland."

"Northumberland," he repeated in some dismay. "That's a goodly distance from here."

"I know," she agreed regretfully. "But it has been decided that I must reside with him."

"When does this move take place?"

"During the first week in May."

"Ah." He smiled his relief. "We've a month and more. You must let me come to call."

"To . . . to call?" she whispered. "No."

"No?" he repeated frowning. "Why not?"

Ceci's helpful lashes covered eyes filled with distress. If he were to call, he would encounter Bella, and in that moment he must forget her very existence! He could not, must not meet her! "My . . . my sister is elderly and very strict. If she were to know that I . . . had met a gentleman . . . . she does not allow me to . . . entertain callers. She would question the circumstances and . . . I should not be able to see you . . . ever again," she improvised, hoping that she sounded convincing.

"That is unfortunate. I should very much like to meet your sister."

"You cannot!" she said strongly.

"My poor child, you are surrounded by dragons, then?"

"Yes," she acknowledged in a small voice, wondering guiltily what Arabella must say if she heard herself described in such terms.

"Yet . . ." His frown deepened. "I cannot like these clandestine meetings."

"No more do I, but—but it must be thus or—or not at all," she said unhappily, yet with a small tinge of excitement. It occurred to her that Bella had appeared in plays which centered on this very situation—though the dragon involved was generally a miserly uncle or a cruel father.

"Not at all . . . is a hard alternative and one I cannot entertain," he said.

"Oh, no more can I." She looked up at him adoringly.

"Miss Gramont . . . Ceci—may I have leave to call you Ceci?"

"Of course you may."

"Ceci, then . . . come this way." His hand was on her arm again.

"Where are we going? To the choir stalls?"

"Not yet. Just away from the shrouded Mr. Donne, whose melancholy features I cannot abide—not at this moment. Let us go into this alcove . . ." He pointed at a spot between two pillars. "You are very small and . . ."

"I expect to be taller. My brother . . ."

"I should hate to see you any taller," he said seriously.

"You should?" she asked, surprised.

"Yes." He nodded. "You are just the right size to stand next to this column and be almost invisible . . . if I stand in front of you."

"Why ought I to be invisible?"

"Because I want to kiss you . . . because I must kiss you before you are two minutes older!"

"Oh, no," she breathed. "You must not!"

"Why not?"

"You . . . you know why," she whispered timorously. "It . . . it cannot be at all proper."

"Have we not decided that we abhor the proprieties?" He stared down into her eyes. "Or are you, after all, afraid of me?"

"I do not know you." she faltered.

"I know you, Ceci. I know you because I've not ceased to envision you since I saw you yesterday in the park. I have lain awake most of the night, thinking about you. I never believed I could be pierced by Cupid's arrow so quickly—but bolts once shot find their targets very soon."

"Oh, they do, they do," she agreed. "It . . . it's like Romeo and Juliet. My sister . . ." She paused, flushing. She had almost confided that Bella planned to play Juliet.

"Never mind your sister," he said. "She's not here to cast stern eyes upon us and"—his lips twitched—"your nurse has conveniently vanished, as well. Please . . . I pray you'll step into the shadow of this pillar."

His eyes were compelling. Looking into them, she seemed to be robbed of all will, all desire to protest. Obediently, she moved backward and felt the cold marble wall behind her. He was bending forward, and raising her arms, she stood on tiptoe to clasp them about his neck—then, her heart pounding, she lifted her lips for her first kiss.

When he finally released her, she felt warm all over, "Oh," she whispered ecstatically. "It was so . . . beautiful. I did not think anything could be so beautiful."

"No more did I," he returned ardently. "Oh, my love, my love, it was beautiful for me, too." He leaned forward again, then drew back hastily. "But I must not . . ."

"Why not?" she demanded disappointedly.

"Because my very dearest, I should not have the strength to let you go."

"I expect you'd better not, then," she agreed solemnly, "for I know I should not want you to let me go."

"Oh, you darling." He laughed delightedly. "I would old Donne had known you."

"I am glad he did not, for then I should have been dead more than a century—and we never should have met at all."

"It was fate brought us together."

"It was a rainstorm," she contradicted.

"A fateful rainstorm."

"Hereafter, I shall always love the rain." she murmured.

"And I shall, too." He moved back and, as he did, his foot struck something. Looking down, he said, "Here . . . what's this?" He picked up her sketchpad.

"Oh, that's mine," she gasped. "I must have dropped it when . . . a minute ago."

"Are you an artist, then?"

"Not an artist. I am only fond of sketching."

"May I see your work?"

She was suddenly reminded of a sketch she had tried to make of him the previous evening. "No . . . there's nothing of interest inside." She reached for it.

"I do not believe you." Moving away from her, he opened it. "Ah—and who is this gentleman?" he glared at her accusingly and strode into the light. "I must see him closer."

"No, please," she begged, darting after him.

"Good God," he exclaimed. "It seems to be myself! And a passable likeness, too."

"It . . . it's not," she disclaimed. "It's nothing like . . . it was done from memory and . . ."

"But it is good," he insisted, looking at her tenderly. "And done from memory was it? Yesterday?"

"Last night."

"You must date it, sign it and give it to me."

"Give it to you?"

"May I not have it?"

"Yes, but . . ."

"Done. We'll trade."

"T-Trade?"

"An artist must have her fee."

"I want no fee . . . and it's not good enough to give."

"I claim it, and in return I shall give you this." He tugged a ring from his index finger and held it toward her. It was of heavy, dark gold, ornamented with a crest picked out in minute diamonds on a shield of red and black enamel.

"No," she protested. "I cannot take it. It must be an heirloom and costly."

"I want you to have it for now . . . later you will give it

back to me and I shall replace it with another sort of ring . . ."
Taking her hand, he slipped it on her largest finger. "Ah,
it covers all the knuckle. It is too big for you."

"I should wear it on a chain . . . but I ought not to have
it . . . that I know."

"You ought not to have my heart, either, but you do,"
he said ardently.

"And you have mine."

"Do I?"

"Forever and ever and ever."

"Then . . . sign my sketch, my dearest love. Do you need
a pencil?"

"I have one." She fumbled in her reticule and brought
it out. "Shall I write . . . 'To Armin'?"

"Write that and if you should want to write more . . . do."

She gave him a shy, tremulous little smile and wrote,
"To dearest Armin, my true love, Ceci Gramont. March
30th, 1806." Handing it to him, she asked, "Does—does
that suffice?"

"It suffices and is far more dear to me than gold." He
folded it carefully and thrust it inside his waistcoat. Leaning
forward, he drew her into his arms. "I must kiss you again."

"Ah, no," she whispered, "there are people approaching."

"Very well." He drew back, saying ruefully, "It seems
I must escort you to those choir stalls."

The stalls, made of beautiful old wood, were elaborately
carved with garlands and with strange faces flanked by
curling plumes, but again, they made little impression on
her. Though she listened dutifully while he explained the
symbolism, if anyone had questioned her on it, she could
have recalled nothing of his discourse. However, if asked
to describe the way his auburn hair curled at the back of
his neck and where the starched points of his shirt collar
grazed his cheeks, or the exact fall of the green scarf he
wore tied around his snowy cravat, or the exact color of his
jacket, or the gold fobs at his waist, or the way his un-

mentionables, tight in the style introduced by Beau Brummel, graced his well-shaped legs, these would have been easy for her to enumerate and even easier would be a catalogue of his features which, she felt, she knew even better than those of her brother George, he having faded in her memory before the vibrant reality of the man beside her.

"Ceci . . . Ceci, where have you been!" Mrs. Moulton's voice boomed in her ear.

Startled, she stared in front of her and saw the chaperon standing some yards away framed in the glow emanating from the dome. "Oh, dear," she murmured regretfully, "I shall need to go."

"But not until you've told me when we shall meet again," he said.

"I . . . the . . . the menagerie in the Tower," she hissed and was glad they were not standing in the vicinity of the famed Whispering Gallery where all sound was miraculously heightened.

"When?" he demanded, his eye on the approaching chaperon.

"Tomorrow afternoon . . . early."

"Are you sure you will be able to come?"

"It has been already arranged," she assured him.

Mrs. Moulton was at their side. "Mr. Sherlay . . . what, you here?" she gazed at him in astonishment.

"Yes, by a most strange coincidence," he said blandly, while Ceci bit her lip against her threatening laughter.

"Strange indeed," Mrs. Moulton marveled. She added sternly, "But you should not have gone off with this young gentleman unaccompanied, my dear. You know such behavior is not at all the thing. I cannot think what your sister will say."

"But I . . . I could not find you," Ceci explained nervously, hoping that Mrs. Moulton would not mention Bella again. She rushed on with her explanation. "When I looked in the chairs, I did not see you."

"Because you had gone," the chaperon returned. "I went to hunt for you. First I looked here in the choir stalls."

"We came here at the last." Mr. Sherlay smiled. "But look you, Miss Gramont is found and all is well."

Mrs. Moulton sighed. "I expect that must suffice—though I cannot approve. Come, my dear, I expect that you have seen enough of St. Paul's."

"Oh, yes," Ceci murmured. "Mr. Sherlay has been kind enough to show me a great deal of it."

"It was my pleasure, Miss Gramont. I am in hopes that we shall meet again."

"I hope so, too." Ceci dimpled.

"Good afternoon, Mr. Sherlay," Mrs. Moulton said coldly.

"Good afternoon, ma'am." He bowed. "Miss Gramont."

"Good afternoon, Mr. Sherlay," she returned. She should have liked to watch him walk across the floor but it was impossible, for Mrs. Moulton nipped at her arm. "I hope you were not too forward with that young man, Ceci," she said worriedly.

"Forward?" Cecil raised wide, questioning eyes. Prevarication, she thought uncomfortably, was becoming all too easy for her, but unfortunately, it was a necessity. "No, but I could not think it wrong for him to show me about the cathedral."

"It was not wrong—if he kept his distance."

"Oh, yes, he did. He is a gentleman. That is certainly evident, I think."

"Yes, it is evident," Mrs. Moulton allowed. "However, sometimes young gentlemen, left alone with young ladies, do not conduct themselves as strictly as one might wish."

"He conducted himself quite as I wished." Ceci was pleased that this, at least, was the truth.

"Well, I must say I am relieved. And...er...Ceci, my dear, I think it were better that your sister were not informed of this meeting, either. It would reflect most badly upon myself."

"Oh, no," Ceci said on a note of relief. "I promise you I shall say nothing."

"You are a good child," the chaperon returned gratefully.

Quite suddenly, Ceci wished that she might tell Mrs. Moulton that she was not a child—that in the space of half an hour she had become a woman, a woman deeply in love with a man who loved her. However, since that confidence was barred, she contented herself with the feel of the ring, still clutched in her hand and which served to lend reality to a situation which was already beginning to assume the lineaments of a dream.

2

"I vow, Sherlay, you are looking damned pensive," said a lazy voice, "and it's your draw."

Sherlay, sitting at a small table in the highly popular gaming club of Brooks, met a quizzical gaze and laughed self-consciously. "I was thinking," he said to the speaker, one Sir Charles Vandrington, a slender man, some four years his senior and dressed all in gray with the exception of his snowy linen and his black, gold-tasseled Hessian boots.

"I make it a rule never to think when I am playing piquet," Vandrington chided.

"Which is why you have won the last three rubbers?" Sherlay inquired with another laugh.

"I make an exception when it comes to the game, but you are giving me scant sport tonight. I like a challenge." His eyes, also gray under brows which like his hair were already silvered, narrowed. "I am adept at reading signs and I should say that yours indicate that you have fallen in love, a pastime I have always deplored as unproductive."

Sherlay started and flushed. "Is it so obvious?"

"Though I pride myself on being reasonably astute, my dear fellow, I should think that your condition was particularly obvious to all save a blind man. Might I know the identity of the fair maiden who has possessed herself of your heart in a little over twenty-four hours—since I could swear that yesterday morning you were not yet afflicted with the 'green sickness'?"

"She is not a *fair* maiden." Sherlay smiled. "At least not precisely—her skin *is* very white and her eyes are blue, but darkly so—while her hair is black."

"Ah, an enchanting combination. I have always found golden locks insipid. Should you call it 'bandying her name about' were you to give it to me?"

"I should not confide it to anyone but you." Sherlay regarded Vandrington affectionately. "For not only are you my first friend in London—I know you to be the soul of discretion."

"'Tis the only soul I do possess, so I thank you for that encomium. What is her name?"

"It ought to be Juliet," Sherlay began self-consciously. "Lord, Lord, I never dreamed it would strike me this way—love, I mean."

"It often strikes you just like that . . . the first time."

"There'll not be another time," Sherlay told him earnestly. "I have quite lost my heart to her."

Picking up one of the small bottles of claret that were on the table, Vandrington poured himself a glassful. "You'll find hearts are retrievable, too." Pushing the bottle toward Sherlay, he drawled, "You'd best drink to that."

"Come, I'll not let you discourage me." Sherlay filled his glass. "I'll drink to love and marriage."

"Love and marriage! Marriage, my dear fellow, and you hardly breeched!"

"We marry young in our family," Sherlay explained. "My mother'd be pleased if I begot an heir."

Vandrington chuckled. "It's rather soon to talk of heirs—you are barely twenty."

"I am the last of my line. My father died young, as you know."

"A short life and a merry one, if I recall."

"Yes." Sherlay frowned. "Short enough, merry enough . . . drinking, gambling, women, and my mother miserable. I'll try not to follow his example."

"Spoken like a Puritan." Vandrington grimaced.

"Spoken like one who does not believe in the curse of the Abbot John." Sherlay smiled.

"Ah," Vandrington's eyes grew intent, as with mock solemnity he quoted:

> "Each Sherlay heir,
> Will badly fare,
> And ere he mend,
> His life may end."

"You've a good memory," Sherlay said in some surprise.

"For bad verse, always. You do not credit that dismal doggerel, I see."

"I am of the opinion that each of us shapes our own destiny."

"Yet . . . from all accounts, numerous Sherlays have lived hard and lasted . . . not long. I must say, however, that I've not noticed that tendency in you. You neither drink nor dice to excess."

"Nor shall I," Sherlay assured him earnestly. "As I see it, many of our family have used that so-called curse as an excuse for wild and licentious behavior. Judging from what my late uncle told me, I am sure that was my father's given reason."

"So . . . out of self-protection, you'll settle down, and instead of wild oats, sow more productive seed."

"It's always been my intention."

"And now you believe you've an intended to match that intention?" Vandrington's tone was slightly mocking. "Do you know—you've not yet confided the name of Juliet?"

"Miss Gramont's parents are dead. She lives with her sister, a dragon of a woman, so I am told."

"So you are told? You've not met her sister?"

"No," Sherlay said uncomfortably.

"You've not been to the dragon's lair?"

"No, we met accidentally both times . . . though I must tell you she is of gentle birth."

"Ummm . . . two meetings in the last day and a half and both accidental?"

"Not on my part . . . you see, after my first encounter with her in Hyde Park, yesterday afternoon, I heard her chaperon say that they'd be at St. Paul's and I knew I must see her again."

"And in this quest, you were aided by her chaperon?"

"Not aided," Sherlay hastened to assure him. "She was talking at random about visiting the cathedral and I overheard her."

"I see . . . and so thither you went to your assignation."

"It was not an assignation!" Sherlay retorted sharply.

"Not on your part, neither?"

"No. She's a charming innocent, I assure you. I could tell that the first moment I saw her. She's little more than a child . . . only a few months past seventeen."

"Some females stop being children at thirteen," Vandrington drawled, fixing an intent eye on Sherlay's face.

"Not this one," Sherlay said firmly. "If you were to see her, hear her talk . . . you'd realize that she knows nothing of feminine wiles."

"I must say I find myself ever more partial to those who do possess some modicum of the serpent's knowledge."

"I have always thought I should, myself, until I met Ceci."

"Ceci?" Vandrington's gaze grew even more intent. "Is that her name?"

"Yes . . . does it strike some chord of memory? I know you have a wide acquaintance among the *ton*."

"You believe her to be of the *ton*?"

"I am sure of it. She's well mannered and well spoken."

"Where does this charming . . . er . . . innocent dwell? In the city, I presume?"

"Near it . . . Chelsea."

"Chelsea." Vandrington shuddered slightly. "That hamlet!"

"It's a pleasant place, is it not?" Sherlay frowned slightly.

"Depending upon what it is pleases you."

"I take it Chelsea does not please you?"

"No, it does not please me. It is not only monstrously out of the way . . . but it is an enclave of chits, artists, and artisans—with a depressing preponderance of the latter. There is also another element whose presence is proving increasingly odious to some of these worthies. I refer to the Aspasias or, as they are sometimes termed, the fair Cyprians."

"Aspasias . . . Cyprians . . . doxies, in fact?"

"Expensive doxies . . . actresses, opera dancers, but I prefer my initial euphemism and so, I think, must you."

"I?" Sherlay stared at his friend with some surprise. "Why should I care what they are called?"

"I am judging from your present state of mind."

"My state of mind?"

"You see . . ." Vandrington chose his words carefully. "The name of Gramont is familiar to me . . ."

"So you said," Sherlay began, then paused, his eyes widening. "You . . . you'd not be suggesting that . . ." He rose so swiftly that the table shook, causing his half-filled glass to tip over, but immediately the claret began to drip onto the carpet, one of the waiters was there to mop it up. Unheeding of the man, he glared at Vandrington, "You . . ."

"Armin." Vandrington was also on his feet and now he put an arm around Sherlay's shoulders. "I beg you'll listen . . ."

"If you are about to. . .to tell me that M-Miss Gramont is. . .is. . ." He shook his head, unable to finish the sentence.

"I am about to tell you what I know about her possible family, though, of course, I might be wrong."

"You are wrong!" Sherlay said explosively and then flushed as several gentlemen playing hazard paused to peer at him through quizzing glasses. He strode toward the door. "You've not seen her. You have n-no c-call to even hint at such a connection. I tell you, she's an innocent."

"If it's the chit I have in mind, she's not been in town long—less than a week, I should say."

"A light for the street, sir." Another waiter stepped forward as the two men approached the stairs leading into the vestibule.

"No." Vandrington waved him away, patting his pocket significantly. "We will be in no danger." He addressed Sherlay. "You will come to my lodgings—you will listen to me and then you will draw your own conclusions—but you must hear me, I think."

Sherlay looked at him, caught between anger and confusion. "How would you know she'd only arrived recently?"

"Ah . . . then it might be she?"

"For God's sake, Vandrington, what do you think you know about her?" They had reached the front portal, and as a footman opened it, Sherlay paused in the aperture, staring over his shoulder at the man behind him.

"My information's not for the ears of any here at Brooks, nor for the lurking footpad. Come." Flinging an arm around Sherlay's shoulders, Vandrington gently edged him out.

In less than twenty minutes, Sherlay stood in Vandrington's small but exquisitely furnished parlor, staring down at his friend, who was casually taking a pinch of snuff. He shook his head as the beautifully enameled box was presented to him. "I want to hear what you have to tell me," he said doggedly.

"If. . . and mind you, I say 'if,' it is the Gramont girl,

she is a daughter of Sir Harry—she and her sister. There is also a brother, but he does not reside in town."

"Might . . . might he live in Northumberland?" Sherlay asked in a low voice and very reluctantly.

"I do not know the location. I only know that he does not live with his sisters. All three of these Gramonts, I might add, are the children of Sir Harry—but begot on the wrong side of the blanket, their mother being an actress named Sophronia Sinclair. The eldest daughter's named Arabella."

"Is . . . she bedridden?"

"Bedridden?" Vandrington laughed lightly. "That, my dear Sherlay, is an interesting way of phrasing it, though I do not believe you were making a play on words."

"I was not." Sherlay said shortly.

"Miss Arabella is not an invalid—she is a very popular young actress. Presently she is playing the role of Polly Peachum at Drury Lane. She lives in a charming little snuggery in Chelsea, provided by her rich protector, Lord Madreston . . . and the *on dit* around town's that her younger sister Ceci has also been taken under his Lordship's wing."

Sherlay was silent a long moment. He stared at the carpet—an Aubusson in a rich gold patterned with fanciful blue flowers. His mind, veering away from that which it hated to contemplate, brought him a memory of Vandrington telling him how he had purchased the carpet from a poverty-stricken émigré family, striking a hard bargain. He had not approved the triumphant note apparent in his friend's voice as he had detailed that transaction. There were other traits in Vandrington which he also deplored. It was a well-known fact that newcomers to the clubs the older man frequented were sometimes enough struck by his eccentric attire to remark on it unkindly, which, more often then not, put them in danger of being challenged. It was hinted that Vandrington's garments were worn for the malicious purpose of seeking duels. A master of both sword and pistol, he always won—often killing his man. Yet, in this instance, Sherlay could detect no malice in his manner, only a determination to protect him from falling into the same error which, Vandrington had hinted more than once, had cast a shadow over his life. A vision of Ceci displaced these gloomy thoughts and Sherlay said, "I cannot think it possible. If you could see her... and furthermore, she has told me that her sister is old and ill."

"Two sisters and a brother named Gramont," Vandrington mused. "And one of those sisters is named Ceci Gramont and is recently arrived in town—Chelsea, if we are to be specific. She is young—sixteen, I believe?"

"Ceci is over seventeen."

"That, too, is young."

"Damn you, I shan't believe it!" Sherlay cried.

Vandrington shook his head. "Save your curses for those that merit them. I am your friend. I speak as your friend and it is as your friend that I invite you to come with me to Chelsea where, as it happens, Bella Gramont will be holding open house. It is her last night as Polly. On Monday next, she will be opening as Angela in *The Castle Spectre*."

"No," Sherlay said positively, "I do not want to go."

"My dear Sherlay, it cannot hurt you to meet a charming beauty. Madreston is also charming. He is always at his best in Bella's company. He dotes on the girl."

"And you suggest that he would undertake to, er . . . dote on her sister, as well?"

"I am sure he is paying her keep until such time as she can find a similar situation. I do not think there is more to it than that."

"Ceci leaves for Northumberland at the beginning of May," Sherlay stated. "She is to stay with her brother."

"I am told that George Gramont is an estate agent for a wealthy friend of his late father's. The name of the family has not been vouchsafed to me. I do not even know if there is a family."

"Enough, I beg you," Sherlay grated. I shall go . . . if only to prove you wrong. I cannot believe that she . . . I

cannot believe it, I tell you. She is not a liar or . . . she's
not!"

"We shall take my curricle," Vandrington said. He fastened his gray gaze on Sherlay's face. "You may not believe
me, but much as you want me to be mistaken, I pray that
I am mistaken. I have suffered at the hands of a clever
female, it is true, but I am not of the persuasion that 'misery
loves company.'"

The music provided by musicians recruited from the Drury
Lane orchestra and the singing of several thespians from
the cast of *The Beggar's Opera* penetrated but faintly to
Ceci's chamber. Though she had yet to doff the blue silk
gown she had worn to the theater and at the festivities
below, she had no intention of rejoining the merry-makers.
She had found them much too loud and boisterous for her
taste. It occurred to her that she never had cared much for
actors. They had such resonant voices. Of course, no one
could blame them for that, when they must needs project
through theaters filled from pit to the topmost gallery with
rowdy audiences which did their best to outshout them.
Then, there were the gallants who moved about on stage
chatting with each other and even with the actresses when
they were in the throes of a performance. Bella had often
complained of the temerity of these young bucks, but there
was no censuring them for they could turn ugly. Last season,
a Mrs. Hunter had been dismissed at their demand and
another had been knocked down and pummeled by one
erratic lordling. "You need to jolly them along," Bella had
confided to her.

Poor Bella, Ceci felt sorry for her. She had looked very
weary after the performance, but Lord Madreston and a
number of his friends had accompanied them home. They
were still there and Bella, with the help of some other
actresses, was helping to entertain them. Ceci, having
glimpsed her sister's harried countenance, guessed that she
was as eager to retire as she herself. She smiled and, catch-

ing her smile in the mirror, erased it quickly. It had seemed triumphant and it had been—she was thinking of Armin Sherlay, whom Bella had not met, would not meet, as long as she could keep them apart. She picked up the heavy gold ring from her dressing table, and sitting on the small stool, she slipped it on her finger—the tiny diamonds in the crest caught the light from the two candles in front of her and sent a host of rainbow-colored specks dancing on the walls. Once more, she was seeing him as he had put the ring on her finger—but even more exciting had been that moment when he had kissed her. Delicious shivers coursed up and down her spine at the thought, or rather, had been coursing up and down all that afternoon and evening. She had been thinking of him constantly ever since she had parted from him in the cathedral—indeed, that night at the play she had not even been aware that the final curtain had fallen until Mrs. Moulton had poked her so that she might applaud her sister.

She smiled ruefully, thinking of the times as a child, when prompted by Papa, she had applauded Mama. That was a very old memory—she had not been in London when her parents had died, Papa first and Mama, less than a year after him. She had seen very little of either parent and she did not think that her brother and sister had had the benefit of Papa's presence in later years. According to Bella, he had been away a great deal of the time. Her mother had been unhappy about that. She had a vague memory of her saying so when she had come to visit her in the house Papa had bought for them in Wiltshire. It was a lovely, large house with a fine garden and stables—but only she, Nanny, and her governess had resided there. Bella was supposed to have joined her, but she had refused as had George. She had never known why—she still did not know. It had not mattered—she had been so busy with her studies. She frowned. After Nanny died, she had been told that the house no longer belonged to herself or Bella and George, which was why she was going to Northumberland. She had asked

Bella about that—she had understood from Nanny that Papa
had willed them the estate, but Bella had only waxed very
cross and told her not to mention Papa's ways to her. She
had sounded as if she had actually hated him, which had
shocked Ceci. She expected it might have something to do
with his partial desertion of their mother.

Her eyes drifted toward the glass and in it she seemed
to see Armin Sherlay standing behind her. "I hope that you
will not remain away from me—once we are wed," she told
that mirrored phantom. "But I do not think you will want
to leave me. I know that I did not want to leave you this
afternoon. It hurt me to be parted from you—even though
I know we shall meet tomorrow. I would like to remain
with you forever. I do hope I shall dream of you tonight—
as I did last night." She jumped, then, for there was a tap
on her door.

"Yes?" she called.

"Child, may I come in?"

Ceci frowned and hastily dropped the ring into her small
jewelry box. It was Mrs. Moulton, whom generally she
never saw at night. "Yes," she replied, annoyed at this
abrupt dispersing of her dreams. "Come in."

As the chaperon entered, Ceci tensed, staring at her in
amazement. Obviously she had been partying with the other
actors, for she was garbed in a gown of russet satin, far too
youthful for one of her years and certainly not enhanced by
the necklace of paste diamonds with which she had decked
her withered throat. More than her garments, it was her
demeanor which was startling Ceci. She was smiling
broadly; she looked actually arch, and if the color on her
cheeks was from a rouge pot, that on her neck was not—
she was blushing!

"My dear, my very dear Ceci, it has happened as I hoped
it would, as I prayed and planned it might—though I think
that dear Bella is quite, quite confused and I thought we'd
agreed . . . But no matter, I cannot think it was wrong of
you to give the direction. Now . . . you must come down.

Bella has asked that you do—as has dear Lord Madreston."

"Bella . . . Lord Madreston?" Ceci questioned. "What can they want with me? I told Bella I wished to retire early and she said I might."

"Yes, but you have not yet retired, have you? Fortunately, most fortunately, you are still dressed and in that most becoming gown. You must come, child. I promise you—you will be most agreeably surprised."

"Surprised? How might I be surprised?" Ceci asked.

"You will see," the chaperon said with the archness that, Ceci thought, went so ill with her hard gray eyes which, she noted, remained harder and grayer than ever, if that could possibly be. Certainly they did not reflect the brightness of her lilting voice. "You will see and you will live to thank me and shall be, I hope, grateful," she said in a tone from which the lilt had abruptly vanished.

"I do not understand you." Ceci told her.

"You will understand, my dear child." Mrs. Moulton had produced the lilt again. "But first let me look at you . . . Stand up . . . stand up . . . ah, now . . ." She stared at her critically. "Yes, that gown is most flattering to your coloring . . . and perhaps some jewelry?" She shook her head. "No, no need to gild the lily. Oh, to be so breathtakingly young again and so many exciting opportunities before you! You will be a success, my dearest. The moment they came in, I knew it. I knew I was right in all I did. The fish snapped at the bait and is fairly hooked."

Listening to her, Ceci bit back a smile. Jackie, who was her late nurse's next to oldest grandson, would have had a word for Mrs. Moulton. He would have said she was "foxed" and, indeed, the flush that stained her neck would indicate that the woman had imbibed a bit too much of claret or, more likely, champagne. Champagne, Bella had told her, had a way of creeping up on you unawares and rendering you very dizzy before you knew it. She did not like champagne, herself. It had a hard, vinegary taste, but the bubbles looked pretty in the glass and she liked the sensation of having them break on her tongue.

"Come, come, come, child," Mrs. Moulton prompted. "You are the greatest one for falling into a dead stupor."

"I am not in a dead stupor," Cecil retorted coldly. "I was thinking."

"Well, you may think later . . . sure you'll have much to think about."

Wonderingly, Ceci followed her out of the room and down the back stairs. Then, at her behest, they crossed to the front stairs and descended into the hall. The laughter and the music, mainly fiddles, were still loud and, as she crossed toward the drawing room, more laughter exploded directly behind her as a young girl, her face imperfectly cleansed of the greasepaint she had worn in the play that night, came running past her pursued by a tall, middle-aged man, who caught her by the door, kissing her most improperly at the bodice. Quickening her steps, Ceci, closely followed by Mrs. Moulton, stepped into the drawing room looking for Bella. She saw her standing near Lord Madreston, talking to a man who seemed entirely clad in gray. With him was another, much the same height as Mr. Sherlay but, of course, it could not be. However, oddly enough, his hair was auburn. Moving closer, she caught her sister's eye.

"Ah, Ceci," Bella caroled in her soft pretty voice, which was as sweet off the stage as it was on. "Do come. I think there's been some mistake . . ."

"No mistake," Mrs. Moulton hissed in her ear, "as your sister will learn before she is an hour older. I tell you . . ."

Whatever else she might have told Ceci was lost as the girl joined Bella and turned to look up at Armin Sherlay. She opened her mouth and then closed it, shock having rendered her utterly speechless. Staring at him incredulously, she was vaguely aware that his companion was smiling triumphantly and saying something, but she did not hear what he said because in that instant she had seen the intense anger in the eyes of Armin Sherlay—an anger so strong it made her feel that it was composed of fire and had burned her. Coupled with it was a look of supreme disgust. Shocked, she took a backward step and then, incredibly, his hand flew out and caught her on the cheek, the while he cried in a voice heavy with tears, "Harlot, harlot, harlot!" and stumbled from the room.

— **Part Two** —

3

THE PARK WAS painted in the colors of mid-October and as the large traveling coach lumbered over the winding road toward Torleigh Manor, Rose Pell, looking out the window saw a tree which was nearly all a bright yellow save for a scarlet splash at the top. "Oh, lovely," she exclaimed and immediately put a hand over her mouth—but, of course, she was too late to stifle an exclamation which had been far louder than she had intended.

Lady Chadbourne, who had been half asleep in her corner of the coach, opened startled eyes. "Did you say something, Rose?" she inquired.

"Oh, Milady," the girl breathed. "I did not mean to awaken you."

"No, matter." Lady Chadbourne's smile was reassuring. "It seems to me I should be waking—we must be near our destination."

"Yes, Milady, we're in the park. It's ever so pretty, now the leaves have turned."

Lady Chadbourne glanced out of the window. "Yes, it's

very pleasant." Closing her eyes, she leaned back against the cushions, one slender hand clutching the strap as she braced herself against the inevitable jolts.

Hearing the weariness in her Ladyship's voice, Rose was suddenly sorry for her. Then, directly upon that feeling, she laughed. It was ridiculous to be sorry for a young woman as wealthy and as beautiful as her mistress. Yet, it was only too apparent that she derived little pleasure from either her wealth or her beauty. In the last few months they had gone from Chadbourne Hall to Brighton to London, and while one would have thought that Lady Chadbourne would have attended the balls and routs to which she had been invited, she had made an appearance at very few of them, spending the greater part of her days either reading, horseback riding, or at the dangerous pastime of gambling. It was true that she was phenomenally lucky, yet she seemed to take little pleasure in winning. In the seven months since she had doffed her widow's weeds, she seemed both restless and dissatisfied.

It was possible, of course that she missed her husband, but Rose could hardly believe that. Though Mrs. Blake, the housekeeper at the Hall, insisted that they had been happy until Lord Chadbourne had suffered his two crippling attacks of apoplexy, it was difficult for Rose to imagine how her mistress could have been compatible with a man over forty years her senior, she having been a mere seventeen when they had wed. Yet, there was no doubt but that she had been a good and patient wife to him—even at the last, when he was no more responsive than a log of wood. She had cared for him as if he had been her child and Mrs. Blake had said it was a great pity Lady Chadbourne had never had a baby. It had been a disappointment to his Lordship, also, for he was the last of his ancient line, his only son having been killed twenty years earlier. Furthermore, if Lady Chadbourne had had a child, she might have been less restless and . . .

The sudden halt of the vehicle brought Rose's thoughts

to an abrupt end. Glancing out the window again, she saw
they had arrived at Torleigh Manor. She sucked in a breath
and slowly expelled it. Though she had been in many fine
houses during her two years with Lady Chadbourne, she
had never seen one that pleased her more. It was relatively
new, not more than twenty or thirty years old, she would
guess. Of a white stone, its wide portico was circled by
Ionic columns and its roof bisected by a small dome. She
found the style ever so much more to her liking than Chadbourne Hall, which was a great barracks of a place, built
in the early seventeenth century and having so many passages and rooms that you were always losing your way. Her
eyes widened and she quickly forgot these annoyances as
she saw the young footman, smart in purple and gold livery,
who had come to help Tom, the coachman and Mark, the
groom, with the luggage. He looked to be a lively lad,
which was a relief after those two old crocks who served
Milady. Meeting his impudent blue eyes and receiving a
wink she chose to ignore, she decided that he might do
much to enliven a stay of a month or more, depending upon
her mistress' vagaries.

Celia Chadbourne, moving up the steps of the portico,
was also conscious of an unexpected lift to her spirits. Un-
knowingly, she was a party to Rose's conclusions, comparing the compact outlines of the Torleigh mansion to
Chadbourne Hall and thinking that the latter was far too
commodious for a childless widow. She had a sigh for that—
she had hoped for a son. She had longed to repay the Earl
for his great kindness to her and she loved children, but she
had proved barren. She shook her head. It was no time to
be thinking about a past one could not alter. She was here
to enjoy herself, not to fall back into the melancholy musing
that had occupied far too much of her time since the Earl's
death nineteen months earlier. There was really no reason
for it—life held new promise and certainly more variety
than she had enjoyed in the last decade. She was no longer
constrained to remain in the company of Gervais Chad-

bourne's elderly cronies and his cousin, whom she had chosen as her companion, did not insist on accompanying her everywhere. She was glad that Miss Dalzell was so biddable because the woman would have been out of place at the Manor—the Earl and the Countess of Torleigh were young, not out of their twenties, and undoubtedly their guests would be of their generation. She had met the lively pair in Brighton the past July and had encountered them again when she had opened her London house in September. They were much in sympathy, being equally addicted to gaming. In addition, she had joined Lady Alys Torleigh for exhilarating rides through Hyde Park. She would have an opportunity to indulge in both pastimes, for she had been invited for the hunting season.

"Celia, dear." Lady Alys, who had been standing in the entrance hall, hurried out on the porch to embrace her guest. She was a tall young woman with curling chestnut hair and sparkling brown eyes. In repose, her features had a classic beauty, but due to the extreme animation of her countenance, many of her friends failed to realize how very lovely she was. Releasing Celia, she looked at her closely. "Have you had a dreadfully tedious journey?" she demanded.

"Not so tedious. We stopped at The Swan as you suggested. It was a very pleasant inn—and so clean."

"Oh, it is." Lady Alys nodded. "But I must advise you that if you feel the least bit weary, do rest before dinner— because we have numerous gentlemen here to pursue the foxes. It seems there's a regular plague of the little beasts about and every hen from here to Cheltenham is in fear of her life. I shall look for you to entertain them—the gentlemen, not the hens. Does that alarm you? I hope not—for we ladies are quite outnumbered and one of us, being already bespoke, diminishes our ranks the more." She gave Celia a roguish look and lowering her voice, added, "I qm quite praying that the lady's husband will not be paying us a surprise visit—but I am assured he is in Scotland seeing to his estates. Still I expect a duel would add a certain *je ne sais quoi . . .*" She paused. "But I am talking perfect non-sense and keeping you out here for naught. Come in . . . I shall have you shown to your room."

She led Celia into a light, bright hall which, again, she preferred to the dark, gloomy entrance of her home. In niches on either side were Greek statues which looked as authentic as those she had viewed at the British Museum. Catching her glance, Lady Alys said with a slight tinge of pride, "Dear Rolf is a friend of Jack Hobhouse, who, as you know, went to Greece with Byron—Byron! The poor man is in such a taking and that Lamb creature scarcely retaining a scrap of her mind. La! What a to-do. But what was I saying? Oh, yes, the statues. Well they were bought for us by Hobhouse . . . they were brought to light in some village or other. They say that marbles are planted like grain in every wheat field throughout Greece."

"So I have heard," Celia nodded. "My husband journeyed to Greece many years ago—he, too, brought back artifacts, but his main interest lay in pottery."

"Oh, yes, I have heard that Lord Chadbourne had a collection of all manner of curiosities and some a museum might envy."

"Yes," Celia agreed. "When I first came to the Hall, I was much amazed by the mummy cases from Egypt and the Chinese screens."

"He must have been a most learned man," Lady Alys remarked.

"Yes, he had wide-ranging interests."

"You must tell us more about them, my dear. I am sure that everyone will want to hear all about the treasures of Chadbourne Hall. Remember I am depending upon you to help relieve that tedium which must descend upon us sooner or later."

Her guest shot her a wary look. In the last few months, she had been aware of various efforts, subtle and otherwise, on the part of her friends to introduce her to eligible gentle-men, this in spite of her oft-expressed determination never to marry again. However, she said merely, "I am sure, dear Alys, that you will be more than equal to the situation."

Lady Alys cocked an eye at her and seemed on the point of arguing but, evidently thinking better of it, she said, "I have put you in the blue chamber. It overlooks part of the gardens. Of course, in this season you'll not be seeing them at their best, but the asters and the chrysanthemums are particularly luxuriant this year."

"That will be pleasant." Celia smiled. "I find autumn flowers particularly to my taste."

"I shall have the gardener send some to your chamber."

"Please no," she protested. "I should much prefer to see them growing in the ground, I . . ." The words froze on her tongue, for a gentleman had strolled through a doorway on her left. He paused on the threshold.

"Ah, Lord Sherlay." Lady Alys' smile was cool. "I should like you to meet Lady Chadbourne."

Stepping forward, he murmured languidly, "Delighted." He took her hand and grazed it with his lips. "I am told you helped make Brighton bearable for Lady Torleigh."

"Indeed she did," Lady Alys said before Celia could answer. "Though she did give me cause to doubt my skill at piquet. However, I have consoled myself with the fact that she is known to possess the Chadbourne Luck."

"The . . . er . . . Chadbourne Luck?" inquired Lord Sherlay, looking at Celia quizzically. "Is that . . . something ancestral, like a curse?"

"It is certainly not a curse!" Lady Alys laughed. "Unless it be on the heads of those with whom she plays. She, as I have learned to my regret, never loses."

"Do you not?" his eyes, half hooded by his lids, widened.

"I have been singularly fortunate, my Lord," she murmured.

"Indeed? I should welcome the opportunity to test my own poor skill against your . . . luck. May I hope that you will deign to give me a game?"

She hesitated, then with a tiny shrug, she said, "If you wish it."

"I most certainly do wish it, Lady Chadbourne."

"Armin! There you are!" A tall, willowy blonde woman came into the hall. Though her features were lovely, her beauty was marred by a petulant frown. "Where have you been?" she continued sulkily. "I have looked everywhere for you."

Lord Sherlay pivoted slowly. "Well . . . and now you have found me." There was a trace of weariness in his tone. "How might I be of service to you, my dear Emily?"

The lady's white hand quivered and Celia had the impression that she quite longed to strike Lord Sherlay. She said, "But we were to meet in the garden. Surely you remember we'd agreed on it."

"Of course I remember and was in the garden not ten minutes since but our paths must have diverged." Though he spoke courteously, there was now no mistaking the languor of his tone.

"I searched for you. I did not see you." She spoke accusingly.

"It is all too easy to get lost in the gardens," Lady Alys said pacifically. "My dear Lady Hammond, I do not believe you have met Lady Chadbourne."

Celia, staring into chill blue eyes, murmured a greeting which was acknowledged with the barest of responses as Lady Hammond turned back to Lord Sherlay, saying with a grimace she evidently imagined to be a smile, "I hope it is not too late to enjoy a stroll through the grounds."

He appeared to consider the question. Then he shook his head. "No, I should say it was not too late, my dear Emily. Come." He offered his arm, which she seized almost convulsively, while Lord Sherlay, with a slight flicker of annoyance in his eyes, said, "Your servant, Lady Chadbourne . . . Lady Alys, I pray you will excuse me."

"Of course," Lady Alys responded. She waited until the

pair had disappeared through another doorway before saying, "I am sorry for that, Celia."

"Why should you be sorry?"

Lady Alys sighed. "I do not know why Rolf always invites him. He finds him amusing. I do not. He is a dangerous man."

"Dangerous? In what way?"

"Ruthless, my dear, the 'compleat Rake.' And he'll not spare you merely because you are a woman."

"Spare me?" Celia's dark blue eyes seemed even darker. "I do not quite understand what you may mean."

"I am talking about your projected card game. He is an excellent player and he takes an almost fiendish delight in winning from anyone who's fool enough to challenge him. I am not at all sure that even the Chadbourne Luck will hold against him. And I must warn you—his stakes are high."

"As are mine," Celia returned, seemingly unimpressed by this dire warning. She pressed a hand against her mouth to cover a slight yawn. "Do you know, Alys, I find that I am rather fatigued and should welcome a rest before dinner, as you suggested."

"But of course, Celia. I should not have detained you so long." There was a worried look on Lady Alys' face. "Please, I pray you'll not encourage Lord Sherlay to play with you."

Celia regarded her with a trace of amusement, "But you have said that we must help entertain the gentlemen."

Lady Alys clicked her tongue. "Have you not been paying attention? I assure you—he is one guest who has entertainment enough already—in Lady Hammond, though I fear he no longer finds her as fascinating as he once did. Pursuers seldom enjoy being a quarry, as she ought to know, but I fear she fancies herself in love with him, silly creature. Her husband's worth ten Lord Sherlays, but never mind that . . . I pray you'll not play games with him."

A strange little gleam lit Celia Chadbourne's generally

somber eyes. "I shall keep in mind all that you have told me, Alys," she promised ambiguously.

Rose, helping her mistress into her peignoir, said, "Is there nothing more you require, Milady?"

"Nothing, Rose. You may go. You need not return until it is time for me to dress for dinner."

"Very good, Milady." Bobbing a curtsey, Rose left the chamber.

Celia heard the click of the latch with relief. She had longed to be alone for the last hour. It had taken all the control she had acquired in the last ten years not to betray by word or look the feelings churning in her breast as she had seen Lord Sherlay come into the hall She was more than grateful that Alys, as was often her wont, had done much of her talking for her. It had given her the time to amass the strength she needed to speak calmly to this man, whom she had not seen for close on eleven years. Despite the changes time had wrought, despite the lines of dissipation and boredom that marked his face, she would have known him anywhere.

She massaged her throat—there was a feeling of constriction in it. Surely her heart was beating faster than usual and she felt cold, no warm—no, she was not sure. She looked longingly at a crystal bottle that stood on the top of the dressing table. She would have given much to send it hurtling across the room. Yet, it was doubtful if the gesture would have assuaged her anger. Indeed, she was surprised by the violence of her reaction. Since she had returned to London, she knew she must encounter him sooner or later, but she had expected it would be at a ball or a rout, where she would be surrounded by other people. Then she might have been better prepared—but something told her that no matter where she saw him, she would have been ill prepared for the rush of fury that had come over her, she who had believed such an emotion was totally beyond her. And in close congress with that feeling were her memories.

Though she would have fain forestalled them, there was no banishing the images that rose to her mind. Once more she was back in her sister's drawing room, seeing him stumble out, his accusing cries still ringing in her ears and her cheek stinging from the blow he had dealt her. Her lips twisted into a mirthless smile. In those days, she had not been furious, she had been hurt, more than hurt, wounded unto death. Indeed, once she had understood everything, including the perfidy of Mrs. Moulton, who had envisioned her in a situation similar to that of Bella and deliberately set out to arrange it, she had fallen into a despondency so great that she had become ill—very ill with a fever that had defied diagnosing. She had wanted to die, but she had not died. She had gone, as planned, to Northumberland—to her brother, who was living in the Dower House of Chadbourne Hall.

Once there, her health had improved but not her spirits. It was in the course of a long desolate walk through the fields that she had met Lord Chadbourne. He had spoken gently to her, endeavoring to coax her out of her depression. He had taken her back to the Hall and showed her his mineral collection, his strange masks from Peru and Mexico, his libation jars from Greece, and his Egyptian sarcophagi. He had taken her up on the roof to let her peer at the moon and stars through his telescope and, gradually, her hurts had healed. She had begun to take an interest in life again, and then, there had come his amazing offer of marriage.

He had not minded that she was nameless; he had gladly conferred upon her his name and his title. Above all there had been his love, not the fervent passion of a young man. He had been gentle, initiating her into the mysteries of marriage gradually, always fearful lest she be frightened or repulsed, but she had been neither. She had been only grateful because of the kindness that had healed the wounds and made life bearable for her. Now she felt as if those wounds had opened again and she was, once more, woeful little

Ceci Gramont being borne back to her room by Lord Madreston.

How angry Lord Madreston had been. He had called Sherlay out. Arabella had told her that—Arabella who had been furious with Ceci because she had feared Madreston might be hurt, but it had been Sherlay, Lord Sherlay, Viscount Sherlay, as she had learned, who had been hurt. Madreston's shot had grazed his arm while his own bullet had gone wild, but honor had been satisfied.

Honor? She smiled derisively. It had been an appropriate gesture on the part of her sister's lover, but it had also been one of his last as far as Bella was concerned. He had not appreciated the contretemps and shortly afterward he had broken with her.

Bella had been briefly shattered, but then she had gone on tour to America, and in Boston she had met and married a wealthy merchant. She had a son. Celia had sent a silver cup to his christening but she was not in communication with the family. Even though she knew the affair to be none of Arabella's contriving, she had been bitterly resentful. Through no fault of her own, she had been ignorant of her heritage, ignorant of her sister's situation, and Lord Sherlay had believed the worst. He . . . she shuddered away from the angers invading her. They had no place in her thoughts. Ten years had passed since she had been Ceci Gramont; she was no longer that silly, loving child. She was Lady Celia Chadbourne and he had not recognized her!

"Have I changed so much?" she marveled. She was taller. In common with George, she had shot up fully four inches before her twentieth birthday—poor George, another unwelcome memory arose to disturb her. Hating his illegitimacy and unable to marry into a respectability that might shroud his origins, he had gone off to fight in America. She recalled his parting words.

"If I have no name, little sister, I'll make one as a soldier. I might even finish as Sir George Gramont."

She and Gervais had argued against his going, but in

vain. The Earl had bought him the commission of lieutenant in the King's Hussars and George, incredibly handsome in his uniform, had sailed for America and death in New Orleans. His loss had been an agony at the time, but nearly four years had passed since then and the pain was only an occasional twinge, nothing to that which she had experienced at the sight of Armin Sherlay as he had strolled into the hall below. Of course, she amended, that was not pain—it was anger, coupled with frustration because he had not known her and therefore could not know that Ceci Gramont, whom he had dubbed harlot, had been for nine years the wife of Gervais Chadbourne, Fifth Earl of Mars.

Moving to her dressing table, she stared into the mirror. Some of her frustration vanished as she studied her image. It was hardly surprising that he had not seen impetuous little Ceci in this poised woman of twenty-six. In addition to her gain of inches, her figure had changed—her bosom was fuller, her body more curved. Then, of course, there was the white lock that streaked back from her widow's peak, vivid and startling against the blackness of her hair. A result of her illness, it was a permanent reminder of that terrible night. There were other changes—her face had been rounder a decade ago; now it had lengthened to an oval and her cheekbones were more prominent. The slant of her eyes was also more pronounced and she was ten years older—too old to dwell on ancient agonies. Yet she could not banish them. Somewhere inside of her, little Ceci Gramont, whom she had thought dead and buried, proved to have been only sleeping and had now awakened. She was calling upon her, Celia Chadbourne, to avenge her hurts.

"He never gave me a chance to explain," she whispered as once Ceci had whispered. "He assumed that I had purposely led him on, that I had schemed to entrap him . . . Why could he not realize that I knew nothing? He should have understood that! He should have known that I loved him!"

Ceci's tears stood in her eyes. She wiped them away furiously, thinking of that man she had encountered in the hall, seeing his hard gaze, his mocking twist of a smile. Alys had called him a rake, cruel to those women who were stupid enough to love him. Certainly he had been unkind to Lady Hammond, who looked to be a cold stick of a creature—but still she did not deserve the cavalier way in which he had treated her. It was a great pity that he could not be paid back in his own coin.

She leaned forward, staring into the glass, seeing her face as he might have viewed it. She was beautiful, she knew that well enough, but her beauty had never really mattered to her. Now, she was glad of it. He deserved a lesson, this man who had almost succeeded in destroying her life. She had noted a flicker of interest in his eyes—it would be challenging to see if she might fan that flicker into a brighter flame and then . . . she was not sure of the "then," but it did not matter, it was the present that concerned her and if she played her cards right . . . cards it would be! Did she not possess the Chadbourne Luck? She smiled, remembering the old saying her husband had taught her. "Those that love luck do not love love—but those who love luck, then love love, lose luck." That was what Gervais had called the secret and the penalty of the Luck, and though it was mere superstition, it gave her confidence, for surely she was in no danger of losing the luck for love of Armin Sherlay.

She moved to the large fourposter and slipped between its lavender-scented sheets. It behooved her to look her very best that night—for weapons, to be effective, must be either well greased or carefully sharpened.

The chamber to which the ladies had retired after the ex-cellent dinner provided by Jacques, who had been appren-ticed in the kitchens at Fountainbleau before the Revolution, was beautiful. Known as the Music Room, its paneled walls were painted apple green and upon its ceiling rosy cupids and muses disported in a sylvan glade. The furniture showed the Egyptian influences of a decade earlier—running to croc-odile-headed sofas and sphinx-faced cabinets. To justify the room's appellation, there was a harp in one corner and a pianoforte against the far wall. Through long French windows, one could see the garden, and at the end of a long, grassy walk a small marble temple glistened white in the moonlight and artfully reflected in a shining pool of water. It was a beautiful view and, by reason of carefully placed candles and the fire glowing on the hearth, the room was filled with a soft light, infinitely flattering to its occupants.

The ladies, six of them and all much of an age, were smartly garbed in the new, fuller gowns which were the rage that season, but though they exchanged small talk, Lady Alys was particularly aware of a sense of strain. She had no trouble tracing its origins. Lady Emily was at fault. She sat a little apart from the others, contributing nothing to the conversation save the smoldering looks that she visited upon Lady Chadbourne, who, much to her credit, appeared utterly unconscious of that concentrated ire. However, it was noticeable that she, also, had little to offer to a conversation that centered mainly on Lord Byron, whom Lady Melinda Grey had once seen in company with his sister, Mrs. Leigh, about whom the most dreadful rumors were circulating. Little Gabrielle Fancourt, Lady Melinda's cousin from France, listened avidly, her small mouth half open in amazement while Lady Coralie Anstruthers looked down her long patrician nose, pretending that she had no interest in the charges of incest which were currently being leveled at Byron and his half-sister. That, of course, was utter nonsense since it was known that she had met the dashing poet and had been quite overwhelmed, subsequently boring all her friends and even her acquaintances with accounts of his charm, his beauty, and his interest in herself. Then, it seemed as if Celia must be drawn into the discussion, for Lady Melinda suddenly commented, "But Lady Chadbourne, you have a slight acquaintance with him, do you not?"

Celia, looking at her bemusedly, said, "I—I beg your pardon?"

Lady Melinda was not put off by this apparent lack of interest. A pretty, dark young woman married to Sir Henry Grey, an avid sportsman, whose talk was all of foxes and hounds, she affected a passion for poetry or rather poets, but only if they were attractive and well-born such as Bysshe Shelley and, of course, Byron. "Lord Byron," she repeated. "It seems to me that someone told me that he had visited you at Chadbourne Hall. Is that true?"

"Oh, yes, shortly after his return from Greece. He had heard that my husband had bought a kylix signed by Epiketos, showing satyrs at play. He wanted to see it and Gervais accordingly asked him to come."

"Oh, my dear, how exciting!" Lady Melinda clasped her hands.

"Did he seem very wicked?" Miss Fancourt asked breathlessly.

"Not in the least. He was most pleasant and extremely knowledgeable about Greece. Even Gervais was impressed."

"Did he stay long?" Lady Melinda demanded.

"Not more than a day and a night. He was off early the following morning."

"Chadbourne Hall," Lady Emily said suddenly, fixing her cold eyes on Celia. "As a child I was acquainted with Lady Drusilla Chadbourne."

"Ah, were you?" Celia inquired. "She was my husband's first wife—a lovely, gracious woman, so I understand."

"Yes." Lady Emily nodded. "*She* was a great lady."

A small, embarrassed silence followed that observation. Its inference was all too clear but Celia Chadbourne seemed entirely unaffected by the determined slight and, again, Lady Alys was pleased by her forbearance. However, she was truly angry with Lady Hammond. Quite evidently jealousy had robbed her of what few brains she possessed just as love had made her a dead bore. Yet, was it love—Lady Alys was not sure of that. It could also have been pride. Emily had been inordinately pleased when Lord Sherlay had

swum into her ken some months earlier. No doubt in the
beginning it had been flattering to have attracted a man of
his reputation. She had dallied with him, then unfortunately
she had succumbed to his charm and she had not been bright
enough to hide feelings patently obvious to everyone save
her husband. At dinner that night, Lord Sherlay, seated
across from Celia Chadbourne, had looked and spoken to
her more than once. That, coupled with Celia's appearance,
had been enough to win her Lady Emily's eternal enmity.

Lady Alys bit down a slight malicious smile. It was
unusual for Emily to feel cast in the shade; she had been
well endowed by nature, but her fair coloring was not so
striking as Celia's darkness, and tonight Celia was looking
her very best. Rose, whom everyone knew to be a veritable
wizard at dressing hair, had drawn her shining locks into
a Grecian knot, fastening a little diamond crescent into that
startling white strand which, rather than detracting from the
beauty of her hair, actually emphasized its vibrant color.
As for her gown, it was a masterly choice, being a black-
and-white-striped satin, very flattering to her figure. Her
jewelry, consisting of a necklace of black lava cameos al-
ternating with large white pearls, caught the eye—especially
when fastened around so white a throat. Matching cameos
dangled from her ears and a strange snake ring coiled half-
way up one finger. Not surprisingly, conversation had
ceased when she had entered the drawing room and five of
the eight men present had immediately gravitated to her
side.

Lady Alys had been pleased that her guest, usually a
little shy, had been both gracious and charming to them all,
but thinking on it, she was also worried—for though Lord
Sherlay had remained aloof from the group around her, he,
seemingly anchored to Lady Emily's side, had glanced in
her direction more than once. It was obvious that he was
intrigued, which, judging by Emily's attitude, might possibly result in the sort of strife every hostess would as lief
avoid. To add to her current unease, it seemed to her that

despite her warnings, Celia did not seem nearly as intimidated as she had hoped. Indeed, she feared she might have inadvertently piqued her friend's curiosity by citing Lord Sherlay's prowess at cards. However, there was always the chance that she could forestall that game by begging Lady Emily to entertain them at the harp. She was a good musician and since one besotted youth had told her that she looked like an angel when seated at the instrument, she had always welcomed an opportunity to perform. "The very thing," Lady Alys, muttered, "to cook geese and forestall fracases." Rising, she made her way to Emily's side.

The strains of the harp resounded through the room, but Celia, tiring of melodies she found too blatantly sentimental for her taste, had unobtrusively slipped away to stand outside in the garden. There was a slight nip in the air but she welcomed it. She also loved the way the moonlight gilded the hedges that stretched on either side of her. The effect was charming. She would have to make a sketch of it so that she might paint it. No—she frowned—she would not do any sketching while she was at Torleigh. There was the barest chance that it might strike a responsive chord in Lord Sherlay's memory—though that was doubtful. She had been worried that, seated directly across from her at table, he might have recognized her—but though he had spoken to her and glanced her way several times, there had been no hint that she was other than a stranger to him—and, indeed, why should there be? How long had they known each other—not even two days!

"But should you not be wearing a shawl?"

Celia tensed and turned to face Lord Sherlay's quizzical smile. "No, my Lord, I am not chilly. I find the air exhilarating."

"I find it exhilarating, too," he agreed, his eyes fixed on her face, "but I feel cheated."

"Cheated?" she repeated on a breath.

"I had hoped we would play cards tonight."

The absurd twinge of panic his words had inspired faded.

"I had hoped we might, too," she said. "Yet, the music is lovely. Lady Emily is a gifted musician."

"Yes, most accomplished," he agreed disinterestedly. "Tell me about this Chadbourne Luck. How did it come into the family?"

"It was supposedly a faerie gift."

"A faerie gift... but those are known to turn into dross directly upon receipt."

"Not if the price is paid..." she murmured.

"The price?"

"Celia, dear." Lady Alys stepped to her side. "I had been wondering where you had gone. Lady Emily's quite weary with playing for us and I wondered if you might not sing."

"Do you sing, then?" Lord Sherlay demanded.

"She does." Lady Alys nodded. "Ballads from the Scottish border—please, Celia."

Ordinarily, Celia would have refused to sing before so large a gathering—she was shy about her voice, it being small and not always true, though Gervais had told her it was admirably suited to the ballads he had loved. However, this time she acquiesced quickly. She was extremely grateful for the interruption. It would leave Lord Sherlay with unanswered questions. She was quite sure he was not used to that. It was also possible that he was not used to ladies who parted from him without the tiniest show of regret. She said in a carefully neutral tone, "Pray excuse me, Lord Sherlay."

"But you must let me turn your pages," he said.

"That is unnecessary," Celia told him gently. "The songs are in my mind. I have an excellent memory, but I do thank you." Without another glance in his direction, she followed Lady Alys inside.

4

THE AIR WAS frosty but the sky was clear and though faintly pink on the eastern horizon, it remained darkly blue overhead, still centered by a milk-white moon with a full complement of stars. In the stable yard, horses whinnyed as gentlemen in pink coats and ladies in dark riding habits were being mounted by grooms who moved among them like so many small dark shadows. Still imprisoned in their kennel, the hounds, massed and eager behind the barred gates, panted, whined, and sniffed the air almost as if they had already caught the scent of the marauding bulldog fox, that bold invader of the hen house, which would be their quarry that morning.

Lord Rolf Torleigh, a husky young man with a shock of straight yellow hair, clad in an orange coat which clashed with the scarlet garb of his companions, sat on a big black hunter, his pale blue eyes bright with anticipation, as he said loudly, "It is understood that we will breakfast at the Smithy midmorning."

"It is understood," one of his friends yelled over a muttering chorus of assent.

Celia, mounted on Juniper, a small chesnut mare, patted the animal's arched neck as it pranced on dainty hoofs, clearly anxious to be off. She herself was equally anxious. She had not enjoyed a cross-country gallop for several months and it was that which drew her—not the hunt. She could anticipate rough terrain, fences, brooks, and ponds and she was already feeling a hint of the exhilaration that only danger can bring. Ever since she had been a mere baby, she had loved the feel of the saddle beneath her and her blood had quickened to the rise and fall of the horse's flanks. "You are just like your papa," her nurse had been wont to say. "And he was a centaur in the saddle."

The old woman, who had cared for Sir Harry when he was little, had described breakneck races across the downs and jumps that few of his friends dared emulate. She smiled wryly. As a child, she had been proud to be like Papa. Then, after she had learned that Papa had not deemed it necessary to bestow his name upon her, there had come a refutation of that inheritance, and for several years she had not ridden. However, one afternoon at Chadbourne, she had made her way to the stables and bade the grooms saddle Trojan, Lord Chadbourne's favorite stallion. She smiled, recalling how fearful and reluctant the men had been. She had been fearful, too, but she had not admitted it, and mercifully, Trojan had been unaware of her trepidation. The old passion had returned, and after that she had ridden nearly every day.

"I vow, Lady Chadbourne, you do have an admirable seat on a horse and I can tell you're not cow-handed." Sir Hugo, a dark youth who had admired her singing excessively the previous evening, rode up to her, his brown eyes full of admiration.

"Cow-handed?" she repeated indignantly, "had you thought I might be?"

"Oh, no, no, no, but some females are, you know."

"What nonsense you do talk, Hugo." Lady Alys had joined them. "As if some gentlemen were not equally cow-handed. My dear Celia, such a love of a habit. You should always wear blue . . . and the turban's most becoming. Is it from Paris?"

"No, I had it copied from one in *La Belle Assemblée*. I liked the fit and I expect I liked the fact that it did not resemble a habit."

"No, it looks more like a walking dress, but will it be hardly enough to withstand the rigors of the hunt? You are bound to be muddied at some of the water jumps."

"It's water-resistant—pelisse cloth," Celia explained. "Oh!" She reined Juniper in as Lady Emily, riding past her, nearly struck the mare's neck with the crop which she was, for some reason, slicing through the air.

"Here, I say!" Sir Hugo exclaimed as the crop did come in contact with his horse, sending the animal forward away from the two women.

Darting a look after Lady Emily's retreating back, Lady Alys said in a low voice, "I'd stay clear of her this morning. She's in a foul temper and, as you cannot help but be aware, she has taken an unaccountable dislike to you. I'd not put it past her to be very unpleasant."

With a tremor of anger, Celia replied, "It were better her unpleasantness were visited upon myself rather than my horse."

"I cannot believe she meant to strike either beast. It was a gesture borne of fustian."

"Good morning, Lady Alys . . . Lady Chadbourne." Lord Sherlay, mounted on a mettlesome white stallion and, perhaps out of deference to his dark red locks, wearing a bottle-green coat, passed them with a nod and a wave as he joined Lady Emily at the far end of the assembled riders.

"I pray he will stay beside her for the whole of the hunt," Lady Alys muttered. "That should restore her smiles and the peace besides. Rolf is . . ."

Whatever she had been meaning to confide was cut off by the sound of the horn. The pack was released, and with what seemed to be one great unanimous bark the hounds were off and the riders streaming through the gates in their wake, some horsemen remaining on the dirt road that wound over the fields toward Cheltenham and others striking out across country. In a very short time Adolphus, the lead hound, had the scent and was in full cry, veering toward a small copse and, in a short time, leading them down into a fertile vale.

The smell of dewy foliage was in Celia's nostrils. The cold wind stung her face. The sky was lighter now, the stars had vanished, and the moon was low in the west. Trees, which had been mere silhouettes, were beginning to display their autumnal colors. The beauty about her, coupled with the fast pace of the mare beneath her, was helping to drive away the unhappiness which had been the inevitable result of her meeting with Lord Sherlay and which the sight of him that morning had reactivated. Momentarily, at least, her projected revenge was in abeyance as she abandoned herself to the immediate pleasures of the chase.

If she had had any qualms about her horse, they were gone after they had leaped the first fence—the animal sailing over it like a veritable Pegasus. Sir Hugo had endeavored to ride near her but at the second jump, a stone wall, his mount stumbled and, to her horror, she saw him fall, but a second later he was up and waving. His steed struggled to its feet, and he vaulted into the saddle again.

The shouts of the other horsemen were in her ears and she urged Juniper onward, while the hounds wound in and out of the woods. They reached a water jump which Juniper, again, cleared easily. A rider behind her was not so fortunate; she heard a splash and a curse, but before she could see who had fallen into the pond, Juniper had borne her through a mass of screening trees and Lady Alys, briefly beside her, cried, "You have been lucky, but there's a hard one ahead—best skirt it."

"I shan't." Celia realized at that moment she had lost her turban, but the annoyance that caused her was swallowed as she approached the next water jump. She was momentarily taken aback by the width of the pool but Juniper seemed almost to float over it, landing gracefully on the verge. In a few more moments she had cleared a rail fence and was out of the woods and into the open fields, side by side with several other riders. Ahead of them, the hounds rushed toward another copse and there came the cry of "Tallyho, Tallyho."

The quarry had been sighted. The hounds were yelping excitedly. Judging from their movements, it would be only a matter of moments before the fox was chopped. Reining in, she turned back the way she had come, meeting some resistance from her mare, but she persisted, riding toward the woods at full gallop, hoping that she might disappear into them before she was seen by the others. She had been glancing over her shoulder and when she turned forward again the rail fence loomed up in front of her almost before she knew it. She was not ready for it. Unguided, Juniper jumped and she felt herself falling. With a gasp, she managed to throw herself out of the way of the animal's hoofs, landing on a pile of dry leaves while the mare, stumbling, righted herself and went on, disappearing into the distance.

Celia lay where she had fallen, not much hurt but winded and willing to remain supine until she caught her breath. She was mainly concerned as to how she might find her way back to the Manor. She had no idea how far they had come, and even if she were to get her bearings, she would be faced with a long walk. Her only hope was that the hunters might return in the direction in which they had come. If they did not, perhaps she could hire a hackney in Cheltenham or some other hamlet. However, the villages were also some distance hence. As she was mulling over other ways to extricate herself from her current predicament, she heard the sound of nearing hoofbeats through the brush. Looking back, she saw that a horseman was approaching the fence. Her first thought that he was not a member of the hunting party was erased when she glimpsed his sun-illumined red curls and his bottle-green coat. It was Lord Sherlay!

"Lady Chadbourne!" he called, leaning forward and evidently looking for her. There was an edge of anxiety to his tone that surprised her.

She sat up. "Here . . ." she called back, remembering in that same moment that she must not appear too certain of his identity. Peering beneath the railing, she said hesitatingly, "L-Lord Sherlay?"

"Yes, ma'am." He had gained the fence and now he dismounted, staring down at her with some concern. "You fell. Are you hurt?"

"No, I landed on these dry leaves." She patted them and they crackled under her palm. "I am only a little shaken."

"Are you sure?"

"I am quite sure. I have learned to relax when I fall." Rising, she brushed the leaves from her habit. "You see, I am nearly in one piece, if you discount the fact that I have lost my turban." She added lightly, "I am glad that I did not follow it, for I fear it went into the water."

He smiled and she noticed that for once the mockery, which she guessed to be habitual in his manner, was missing. With a pang, she found he looked younger, more like the boy she had once encountered in the rain. It was an image that fortunately vanished as he drawled, "I am all admiration. I had expected vapors if nothing more."

"I am not a female who indulges in vapors."

"That is obvious."

His gaze, lingering on her face, struck her as singularly piercing and again she was wary, wondering if, after all, he was trying to place her in some niche of memory. Her sense of unease increased when, belatedly, she realized that she did not know why he was there at all. She dared to say, "I am surprised that you knew I'd met with an accident, my Lord."

"I saw you turn back," he explained, "and I wondered

if you might be ill. I followed and saw your mare go off riderless. Were you ill?"

"No." She wondered what she might say by way of explanation and decided that truth must suffice. "You will think it very odd of me but I am loath to see animals—even foxes—slain. No doubt you must be surprised that I join the hunt at all. I can only say that it's because I enjoy the course if not the conclusion."

He regarded her for a long moment before saying slowly, "You are quite amazingly honest."

"It's kind of you not to tell me that I am also amazingly foolish."

"I do not deem it foolish to avoid being in at the kill if such sights turn you queasy."

"They do not turn me queasy. They only distress me, even though I am aware that foxes must be destroyed."

"Yes, and this one's thought to be old and cunning, a thorough villain—well stuffed with stolen poultry." Tethering his horse to a fence post, he slipped through the railings to face her. "You must let me take you back to the Manor, unless you'd prefer to await the others at the Smithy."

"No, but . . ." she began.

"Good," he interrupted quickly. There was a gleam in his eyes. "If you are not too bruised, I should very much like to test the potency of the Chadbourne Luck . . . or do you find yourself too weary to play?"

She hesitated—mainly because she was having some trouble in downing the laughter that threatened to escape her. She had, she realized, been on the point of believing him more considerate than his reputation indicated. However, rather than being concerned over her possible illness, his main reason in following her had been the hope that he might inveigle her into a card game which, she was positive, he believed himself entirely capable of winning. Regaining her composure, she said, "I am not weary, Lord Sherlay. I should be delighted to put the Luck to such a test."

His smile broadened. "I thank you. Come." Helping her
over the fence, he lifted her onto the horse with an ease
that surprised her. As he swung up behind her, the irony
of the position in which she found herself brought a derisive
smile to her lips. How Ceci Gramont would have thrilled
to his nearness. Lady Celia Chadbourne, feeling Ceci's
beloved slip a sustaining arm around her waist, thought
only of the projected card game and prayed that the Luck
would bring her some part of the revenge she desired so
fervently.

The sun, nearing its zenith, shone through the long windows
of the library at Torleigh Manor. Celia, sitting across from
Lord Sherlay at a small table, blinked as the bright light
glittered on the surface of the golden coins he was pushing
toward the growing pile at her side. "Rubiconed, by God,"
he exclaimed ruefully. Leaning back in his chair, he regarded her with amazement. "That, my dear Lady Chadbourne, has never happened to me in all my years of play.
Am I to attribute my successive defeats to the Luck or
acknowledge that you possess a greater skill than any I have
encountered?"

"I leave the choice to you, my Lord," she said demurely.

A smile, amazingly devoid of rancor, played about his
lips. "For my poor pride, I should prefer to attribute it to
the Chadbourne Luck, but I have never countenanced the
superstitions by which crestfallen losers comfort themselves. I shall console myself only with the fact that you
must have had a superior teacher and many hours of prac-
tice—as well as an astute mind."

"I cannot say whether or not my mind is astute, but I
did have a fine teacher in my husband and we passed many
nights at piquet."

His eyes, more green than hazel in the sunlight, dwelt
on her face. "I am inclined to believe that those hours had
been better filled with different instruction."

Suppressing a gasp at his audacity, she said blandly, "I did have different instruction, my Lord. He also taught me whist, hazard, faro, backgammon and other games."

"He must have been an extraordinary man," he marveled.

"He was."

He looked at her for a long moment and then he said almost curtly, "I pray you'll give me leave to recover my equilibrium before we resume the play?"

"Of course," she assented. "If you are of a mind to continue."

"Are not you?"

"I am."

"Good." Rising, he stared down at her. "It's passing close in here. Should you care for a stroll through the gardens?"

"That would be pleasant," she agreed.

"Come, then." He offered his arm and with the barest hesitation, she took it.

Save for the moment when she had stepped out of the drawing room the previous evening, she had not been in the gardens. As Lady Alys had said, autumn had invaded them but the chrysanthemums were beautiful—a planting of great bronze and gold flowers gave way to shaggy white shasta daisies and then to tiny purple blossoms which she knew to be an Oriental variety of the same family. There were also starry white marguerites and bright yellow asters. None of these were rigidly confined to beds, but instead, massed together in wild abandon beneath carefully clipped hedges. "Oh," she breathed, "it is well done . . . such colors!"

"You seem to love flowers," he remarked.

"Oh, yes."

"My mother was also fond of them. Her garden was her chief delight."

"As has been mine." She smiled. "It is very rewarding to plant seedlings and see them come up in their seasons, justifying all your hopes for them."

"My mother was fond of roses."

"They are lovely, but all flowers are lovely." She knelt to examine a bed of pale lavender daisies.

"Still, I think that as a garden enthusiast, you must enjoy the spring the most."

"Every season has its blessings."

"Indeed? You must indeed be an optimist, Lady Chadbourne."

She kept her eyes fixed on the flowerbeds, knowing that in their depths lay an irony to equal that which she had caught in his tone. "I am talking of gardens of course," she explained.

"Good, I approve your qualification. Might I know where your garden lies?"

She rose. "At Chadbourne Hall—near Haltwhistle."

"Border country, then?"

"Yes."

"That was why your late husband was so enamored of border ballads?"

"There was a closer connection than that. You see . . . Chadbourne Hall was built on a site once occupied by a Norman castle—built by the first Chadbourne. He was created a baron by William the Conqueror. His son was engaged in border raids, and though his quarry was generally limited to sheep or horses, he once brought back a daughter of the Dalrymple family and kept her prisoned in the keep until she agreed to wed him. There was a ballad written about it, which my husband's nurse used to sing to him. It whetted his interest in the whole of the literature."

"It seems to have had a happy ending. Most ballads are more realistic—finishing with the lover murdered by avenging clansmen and the lady dying of grief."

"Can you think it realistic to die of grief?" she inquired softly.

"I expect I should have said tragic rather than realistic."

"And I would call it foolish rather than tragic. If one

love dies or is lost, surely there's always another to replace it."

"Ah, your wit belies your appearance, Lady Chadbourne."

"My—appearance?"

"One does not expect beauty to be cynical."

"I fear you must measure all women by a single yardstick, my Lord."

His eyes widened and then narrowed as he stared at her speculatively. "If I have fallen into that regrettable habit, you have convinced me that I am in error."

"Indeed? I must consider that a victory."

"And not your first of the morning." He laughed. "Still in spite of my two miserable defeats, I find that our jousts have brought me rare sport. I could wish you'd emerged from your Northern fastness sometime sooner. What was it kept you there? Gardens?"

"And my husband," she said.

"Was he such an ogre, then?"

She shook her head. "He was the kindest man I ever knew."

"I am sure he had no reason to be other than kind."

She dared to look him full in the eyes. "One does not always need a reason to be unkind, Lord Sherlay."

"I hope that knowledge has not been culled from experience."

"From . . . observation, my Lord."

"Why have we never met before?" he demanded abruptly. Then, before she could answer, he continued, "Have you always dwelt near the Scottish borders?"

"Most of my life."

"And were you born there?"

It was on the tip of her tongue to tell him she had come there when young, but she decided it was less complicated to lie. "I was born on the island of Lindisfarne." she said. She had selected that spot because it was tiny and seldom visited, though, she realized belatedly, there was always the chance he might have gone to see its ancient abbey.

His laugh, unexpectedly boyish, startled her. "It seems I am forever being told of places I did not know existed."

Relief drew an answering laugh from her. "In that part of the country, it's London that has no existence."

"Lord, Lord, you must have been raised among savages. But I am told you have a house in London."

"That is true."

"Might I hope you'll be there for the season?"

"I have that intention."

"Might I call on you?"

Excitement thrilled through her. With very little effort on her part, he was responding exactly as she had hoped he might. She said casually, "Of course."

"You must give me your direction and . . ."

"Armin!"

As his name, uttered in Lady Emily's shrill annoyed tones, reached Lord Sherlay, he stiffened and turned to face her as she came toward them. Evidently she had just returned from the field, for her hair was disordered and her habit splattered with mud. Ignoring Celia, she confronted him furiously. "Where did you go?" she demanded.

"Since you see me here," he returned coldly, "I need hardly explain."

"Why did you leave me on the field?"

"It was not a question of leaving you, my dear. Lady Chadbourne met with an accident."

"An accident?" she snapped.

"I was thrown and my horse bolted," Celia explained.

Lady Emily's ice-blue eyes traveled the length of Celia's body. "I do not see that you are any the worse for your experience, Lady Chadbourne."

"Fortunately, I was not much hurt. Though I am most indebted to Lord Sherlay. If he'd not brought me back to the Manor, I must surely have lost my way."

The high titter of laughter that greeted her explanation

grated on her ears. Lady Emily's tone was studiedly insolent. "I doubt that, Lady Chadbourne. I think you are perfectly aware of the way you wish to go—at all times."

Celia saw Lord Sherlay's eyes blaze, but before he could speak, she interposed quickly. "It's kind of you to say so, Lady Hammond, but I think you credit me with a better sense of direction than I actually possess. Now, if you will excuse me?" Without another look at either of them, she went back across the gardens and into the house.

She was pleased to find the hall deserted and even more relieved to encounter no one on her way to her chamber. There was a chaise longue by the fireplace and she sank down upon it gratefully, glad, too, that there was a fire crackling on the hearth. She was chilled and unexpectedly weary, sensations she did not hesitate to ascribe to a relaxing of the control she had been obliged to exercise while in Lord Sherlay's company.

With a wry little smile, she decided she could compare her emotions to water, once heated, then left to cool, only to have a second fire kindled beneath it. The anger and the resentment that bubbled up in her mind were fully as hot as they had been when in the grip of that earlier conflagration, but there was one great difference—Ceci Gramont had given her heart to Armin Sherlay. Celia Chadbourne despised the man he had become. He was heartless and irresponsible. She was sure that he found Lady Emily's chagrin at his disappearance from the hunt merely wearying, the while he accepted her adoration as no more than his due. Certainly, the woman was most unpleasant, and despite her beauty, Celia was at a loss as to understand what had brought him to her side in the first place. It might be, she decided, that she had presented a challenge. She was obviously proud, haughty, and, from her general demeanor, seemingly unapproachable. To have laid siege to this fortress and secured its surrender must have given him a perverse pleasure. She imagined that having achieved his victory and planted his flag, his interest must have waned quickly. That did not excuse his subsequent indifference, his casual cruelty. Unwillingly, Celia could compare that lady's anguish to that which she had suffered all those years ago. Indeed it was a pity that she might not tell her that if she, Celia Chadbourne had her way, this particular gander would have his fill of a very sour sauce!

Having reaffirmed her vow, Celia settled down on the puffy satin pillows of the chaise longue and was asleep within seconds. Much to her surprise and anger, she awakened with a distinct memory of dreaming that she was young Ceci Gramont, clutching the arm of an equally youthful Armin Sherlay as they hastened through a rain-drenched park with Mrs. Moulton in hot pursuit, shrilling scolding them. Once aroused, she realized that the scolding voice was still in her ears. Looking toward her chamber door, she saw that it was slightly ajar and that Rose was standing close beside it, peeping through the narrow aperture.

Celia was about to call her when a spate of angry words reached her. "Yes, I am going and I will thank you to have my coachman bring the chaise around." The voice was that of Lady Hammond and it was choked with fury.

"But Emily"—it was Lady Alys, who was speaking, half in concern, half in annoyance—"It's growing dark and the roads . . ."

"Damn the roads! I'll not stay another moment under a roof that shelters the pair of them."

"Emily"—Lady Alys's voice had turned chill—"you mistake Lady Chadbourne. Her horse came riderless back to the stables."

"And I am sure she sent it there. She's an artful, designing minx. I knew it directly I laid eyes on her. A woman young enough to be Gervais Chadbourne's granddaughter is heir to all his lands. He must have been in his dotage when she lured him into marriage."

"You've no call to say that. You know nothing about it."

"No more do you," Lady Emily retorted. "I tell you—

she's an upstart and a commoner and . . ."

"That is quite enough, Emily. She is my friend and my guest. If you were sensible, you'd know well enough where to fix the blame for Lord Sherlay's defection."

"He was mine until she . . ."

"Emily," Lady Alys interrupted, "you are sadly deluded. However, I shall have the chaise brought round."

Celia's fists had clenched and for one wild moment she wished she were a man so she could call Lady Emily out and run her through—but anger was swiftly replaced by uncertainty. In encouraging Lord Sherlay, she had made an enemy—one who was, as Lady Alys had said, deluded and, would, Celia was sure, for her own pride, remain that way. Lady Hammond was too full of self-consequence ever to realize that it was she and she alone who was to blame for the lessening of Lord Sherlay's interest—nor would she remember that the situation had worsened even before she, Celia Chadbourne, had ever appeared on the scene. She was also uncomfortably positive that Lady Hammond would not fail to air her dislike to various interested members of the *ton*.

Suddenly she felt alone and stripped of the protection she had enjoyed for the last decade. Without Gervais at her side, she was Ceci Gramont again, the nameless waif who had been briefly sheltered in the house of her actress sister, who was also well known as Lord Madreston's mistress. She had a wild impulse to leave that very night and return to Chadbourne Hall, where she, like those uprooted giants of Greek mythology, who found their strength only in earth, could touch the grounds where she had found her own first foothold. However, even as that craven desire flickered in her mind, she dismissed it furiously. Actually, she was fortunate that Lady Hammomd was leaving; it gave her a clear field to further her own designs and she would not need to tax herself as to her rival's discomfiture. As she reached this conclusion, she saw that Rose had closed the door. Quickly, she shut her eyes. It would not do to let the girl know she had heard the altercation in the hall.

"Milady . . . Milady . . ." Rose, standing at the foot of the chaise longue, called softly.

Celia achieved a slight start. Opening drowsy eyes, she asked, "Is it morning already?"

"Morning?" Rose questioned in surprise. "Oh, no, Milady, it be no more than five in the evening."

"Oh." Celia blinked. "I must have been very deeply asleep." She sat up and as she did she felt a slight twinge of pain and knew it to be a reminder of her fall. Though it had not hurt much at the time, certain reactions were bound to set in. She would probably be a little stiff the next morning, though from past experience, she knew that little in the way of actual discomfort would result. However, if she were slightly incapacitated, that might add even more credence to the tale of her mishap, if such credence were necessary. With a moan, she sank back among her pillows, "Rose, I . . . I find I am aching all over. I was thrown, you know."

"Oh, yes, Milady, I heard. I do hope you wasn't hurt badly." There was just the suggestion of a twitch at the corners of Rose's mouth, but her reaction convinced Celia that Rose, full as she was with Lady Hammond's loudly expressed woes, might be inclined to credit her mistress with duplicity.

She made an effort to rise, then shook her head. "I do not understand it. I was well enough before I went to sleep, but now I am very sore. I fear you must give my excuses to Lady Alys. I do not believe I should go down to dinner."

"Oh, Milady." Now Rose was all concern. "I am sorry." Hastily she helped Celia to her feet and quickly undressed her for bed.

Once she was alone again, Celia's lips twitched into a rueful smile. She was being quite as artful as Lady Hammond believed she was—but there was no help for it, not if she were to achieve her ends.

5

IT WAS NEAR midnight and the candles in the drawing room had burned low. Talk was muted. Earlier, there had been a table of whist and another two of piquet. These games at an end, the guests had either retired to their rooms or were seated near the fire with their host and hostess. Sipping canary wine and occasionally darting surreptitious glances at Lady Chadbourne and Lord Sherlay, Gabrielle Fancourt, seated next to Lady Melinda, said finally, "*C'est affreux*, I do believe she is winning again and for the third straight night. It is almost as if *le diable* were at her shoulder."

"It is not frightening." Lady Melinda laughed softly. "I assure you, *ma petite cousine*, her devil's a good memory."

"I, myself, prefer to credit the Chadbourne Luck," Sir Hugo whispered with a wink.

"That, dearest Hugo, is because you do not believe that females have any proper card sense." Lady Alys tapped his silk-clad knee with a reproving fan.

"Exactly." Lady Melinda's glance was challenging. "I

think Lord Sherlay's fallen into that same error and it's rendered him careless."

"How handsome he is . . ." breathed Miss Fancourt. "If I were playing, I should want him to be my . . . conqueror."

A chorus of quiet laughter greeted her statement and Lady Melinda, shaking a jeweled finger at her, said knowledgeably, "You would succeed only in boring him. It is, I am positive, a new and intriguing experience for his . . . handsome Lordship to be bested by a woman, especially since he holds all females in such contempt."

"Contempt? Does he? He has always been most polite to me." Miss Fancourt's brown eyes grew wider.

"You are a mere infant and his Lordship does not concern himself with children."

"I am not so young." Miss Fancourt pouted. "And she is old."

"Old?" Lady Melinda echoed. "You are daft, my dear."

"Does she not have white hair?"

"Yes, she does and would that I did, too." Lady Melinda toyed with a lock of her own dark hair. "Yet I am sure that bleach would not suffice."

"I hope that Sherlay does not compensate for his losses by attempting to win in another territory," Lady Alys murmured to her husband.

"You do him wrong," he reproved. "He'd not seek such reprisals. He's a good loser. He's a good man in many respects."

"Except with women," she insisted.

Lady Melinda, a party to their whispered conversation, said, "He might have met his match when it comes to Celia Chadbourne. She is certainly no Emily Hammond to fall into his grasp like a ripe plum."

"Nor was Emily . . . not in the beginning," Lady Alys reminded her.

Sir Hugo's smile had vanished. He darted a sharp look at Lord Sherlay. "Lady Chadbourne's not without her protectors," he said meaningfully.

"And," added Lord Rolf, "I am not at all sure that she is in need of protecting. She's an amazingly self-sufficient young woman."

Armin Sherlay might have echoed that conclusion as he looked across the table into eyes which returned his glance steadily but with an expression he found oddly enigmatic. Particularly surprising to him was the absence of the elation which any gambler, male or female, might be expected to experience after a gain of five thousand pounds. There was, he thought, something unsettling in her calm acceptance of her victory. There were other facets of her personality which he found equally disturbing.

On the day of the accident, he had thought he had discerned something provocative in her manner. He had toyed with the idea that she might have, as Emily had so furiously insisted, deliberately set out to ensnare him. However, he had been reluctantly forced to concede himself in error. Far from encouraging his attendance, she had actually avoided him. She had seemed, in fact, to prefer the company of that vapid young man, Sir Hugo Clavering or his equally vapid crony, Lord Randonell, or indeed, any of the other men who clustered about her like flies. On such times as he had ridden near her during the hunting, she had been pleasant but cool. To a man whose conquests were usually achieved so easily that boredom was like to set in practically at the moment of surrender, he was at first irked, then angry, but now he was puzzled and uncertain.

Though he hardly cared to acknowledge it, even to himself, though he had a deep prejudice against females of her coloring, he had been attracted to her directly he had seen her in the hall that first day. He was hard put to explain that attraction. She was beautiful, but it was not her beauty alone that intrigued him, nor was it her intelligence. There was that about her which hinted at unexplored depths and of a slumbering passion that, once awakened, promised an excitement he had yet to experience. Indeed, his so-called eagerness to test the Chadbourne Luck had been a ploy, instituted because he had hoped, in the course of play, to probe further into her mind. Yet, after sitting across from her for the better part of three evenings, he had found his attempts at gaining a greater intimacy gently but firmly foiled. She did not encourage conversation during play and afterward she limited herself to mere generalities. Consequently, he knew little more about her than he had learned that afternoon they had strolled in the garden. Also he had the unwelcome suspicion that, as his losses increased, her interest in himself had decreased proportionally to the point where it bordered on indifference. His jaw clenched and the hand that was not holding his cards curled into a fist. Much to his surprise, he longed to strike her for at least that most ungentlemanly action would bring him forcibly to her attention. His surprise changed into amazement; it had been years since he had been so doubtful of his prowess, years since he had found a woman who attracted him as much as Lady Chadbourne—Lady *Celia* Chadbourne, whose very name should have prejudiced him against her—Celia . . . *Ceci*.

He shuddered away from that yet pervasive memory, that disillusioning moment which had altered his whole life, had shown him that Vandrington was right. He had fixed his attentions upon an artful young Cyprian—his lip curled—what was more commonly known as a "fashionable impure."

"But she was so young," he had cried out of his agony to Vandrington and much as Virgil had led the poet Dante beyond the gates of the inferno, so Vandrington had escorted him to various sequestered hostels where maidens from ten to thirteen had solicited his favors. He smiled mirthlessly. She . . . but why was he thinking of Ceci Gramont after all these years? She was an old ghost now, as insubstantial as the imprint of a hot breath upon a window pane. He looked at Lady Chadbourne, who in that instant was laying down her cards—amazing to realize that so many thoughts had sped through his mind in that instant, all activated by the lovely young woman opposite him. However,

he must not let her disturb him any longer. "Well," he
drawled, "you've bested me again, Lady Chadbourne."

"Yes, but not without a battle," she said kindly.

He resented the kindness. "Would you be trying to console me?" he inquired softly. "As a one-time soldier, I can
tell you that it's not the single skirmish determines the
victory, it's the overall skill of the general, as you have
proved far too often for my peace of mind."

Her eyes widened. "You have been a soldier?"

"Does that surprise you?" Celia detected a faint note of
chagrin in his voice as he continued. "No doubt, you think
of me as a frippery fellow, but yes, I saw some action on
the Peninsula."

She *was* surprised. She had thought of him as passing
the intervening years solely in the pursuit of pleasure. She
said, "You must have been in great danger. Were you in
many battles?"

"No, I sustained a trifling wound and was sent home.
Once there, I decided I'd seen enough of Portugal and so
resigned my commission." He shrugged.

She was glad he had enlightened her. She had not wanted
to admire him and now he had obviated the necessity. In
common with such so-called officers as Beau Brummel,
who had resigned his captaincy in the Tenth Dragoons
merely because the regiment had been posted to Man-
chester, she imagined he had joined up as a lark. How much
different had been the attitude of her brother, who, in addition to his ambition, had been fired with patriotism. In
that moment, her projected plans concerning the ultimate
discomfiture of Lord Sherlay took on even greater dimen-
sions. Not only she but George, and yes, even Bella, would,
in a sense, be avenged for all they had suffered at the hands
of these cruel, careless members of the *ton* and not in the
too-distant future, for it was apparent to her that her coldness
had intrigued her quarry. She had secured his interest for
the nonce, but if she were to retain it, she must take such
risks as the one she had planned that morning.

"Lady Chadbourne . . ."

She started slightly. In contemplating her strategy, she had actually forgotten that its object was sitting across from her. "Yes . . ." Her glance was deliberately vague.

He said intently, "Where had you gone?"

"Oh." She let her eyes wander past his face. "I was . . . thinking."

"That was obvious," he said with the suggestion of a snap.

She gave him a small conciliating smile. "I fear I have been unmannerly, but there's so very much I must do before returning to town tomorrow morning."

"You are returning *tomorrow?*" He frowned. "You've been here less than a week."

"I know, and no doubt you will believe I should not go now, while I am at the crest of my luck, but I must." She looked at him appealingly. "I have promised my late husband's man of business to confer with him and . . . but I cannot begin to enumerate all that compels my return."

"You should not be burdened with so many responsibilities."

"Oh, I welcome them. It makes me feel closer to Gervais somehow."

"Fortunate Gervais . . ." he murmured.

"Fortunate?" She was momentarily taken aback. "But he is dead."

"Fortunate that he merited so much of your love during his lifetime and so much dedication after his demise."

"I have much reason to give him both."

"Oh, more than fortunate Gervais." He smiled. "I had thought faithfulness had gone out of fashion."

"In London, perhaps, but you see, Lord Sherlay, my husband and I were much in the country."

"I hope that you are not suggesting that had you been in town, you might have yielded to its temptations, Lady Chadbourne."

"Such a suggestion had not even crossed my mind, Lord Sherlay."

He sighed, "It is a pity you are leaving when there is yet so much I might learn from you."

"It must be." She smiled. "Now I hope that you will forgive me if I bid you good night."

He rose quickly, extending a hand to help her to her feet. "I wish you would remain another day."

She shook her head. "It's not possible."

"Then, I must have your direction."

"Of course, it's Chadbourne House, just off Grosvenor Square on South Audley Street."

"Ah . . . that is very near the park. Might one hope that you will either drive or ride with me in the park?"

"If it does not rain, I should be delighted," she answered boldly, and under the veil of her lashes she studied his expression.

He smiled. "I might not have been fortunate at cards, Lady Chadbourne, but I shall try another form of gambling. I shall enter a bet at Whites that on the day I choose, it will not rain."

Once more, she was reassured. No memory of Hyde Park in the rain had come to trouble him at her words, and indeed, why should it, after all these years? She said, "Against whom will you make this wager?"

"Against the heavens, Lady Chadbourne, and I shall pray that by the time I am back in London—the onus of the Chadbourne Luck will have ceased to cast its shadow over me."

"Well, I confess myself all agog to hear of this wondrous female, who not only wrested a great deal of the ready from you, but who succeeded in bringing you back from Torleigh a week earlier than you had anticipated." Sir Charles Vandrington stared down at Lord Sherlay—then, as was his wont, he opened a small onyx snuffbox, tipped some of the mixture onto the back of his hand, and sniffed.

Lord Sherlay, seated at table in the paneled breakfast room of his house on Cork Street, carved himself a slice of beef before answering. There was an edge to his voice when he finally inquired, "Where had you all your information, Vandrington? Not from any Parisian source, I fancy."

Vandrington's eyes, bloodshot from a night at Boodles, were full of malicious laughter. "It was the fair Emily, whom I encountered at Hyde Park Corner yesterday evening. You no longer seem high in her esteem, my dear fellow. Yet, I must say that you escaped with a better reputation than did the lady."

Sherlay's brows drew together. "Fortunately, I think there'll be few who will heed her."

"You may be certain of that. It's only too obvious that it's spleen occasions her invective. A tiresome creature. I cannot think why she attracted you at the outset—the lure of the forbidden, I expect."

"If only she had been completely forbidden." Sherlay sighed.

"I pray you'll not repine, for had she, you might yet be at her rather large feet. Talking about feet, do you kneel before those of Lady Chadbourne, or do you but bide your time until you can grasp some more felicitous part of what I hear is a most charming anatomy?"

"And where did you hear that, Vandrington?" Sherlay's eyes had narrowed and his mouth was grim.

Vandrington hesitated. "I am racking my brain . . . it was . . . ah, yes, Sir Hugo Clavering, who wandered over to the hazard table this morning—though I must assure you that I was speaking but figuratively. I do not believe the fair enigma has granted him any untoward privileges. Indeed, I should think it quite the contrary, which suggests that she is gifted with discernment as well as luck—if indeed it is luck and not manipulation."

"It is not manipulation. I am no flat. She won by fair means."

"Fair is foul and foul is fair . . . when one's mind is befogged by beauty—at least in my experience."

"You do speak a lot of nonsense, Vandrington."

"I am glad if it is nonsense. Lady Emily notwithstanding, the Chadbourne seems to be a female of many parts, yes?"

Though Vandrington had lost nothing of the charm that had had so much appeal for Sherlay in his early youth, he was finding the manner of the man he still considered his best friend singularly annoying that morning. However, it would not do to let him have any inkling of that annoyance. He was not in the mood to parry the barbs that must inevitably be visited upon him. Furthermore, Vandrington, who remained an avowed critic, not to say enemy, of the fair sex, would not hesitate to apply his wasplike wit to the lady, as well. From past experience, Sherlay guessed he was primed for it. Though he had often been highly amused by the older man's sallies, he was strangely reluctant to have them loosed upon Lady Chadbourne. Still, since Vandrington's curiosity must be at least partially assuaged, he said as casually as he could, "I presume you have been sent a card to the Carlton House ball this evening?"

"I have, though I'd little thought of attending. With poor Brummel removed to Calais, there's scant entertainment round the Regent—unless you count his figure."

"Well, if you should change your mind, you'll be able to meet Lady Chadbourne and form your own conclusions about her."

"Ah, then I must go. I am all expectation for sure it must be a *rara avis*, indeed, who has the power to stir your jaded senses."

"I did not say that she had," Lord Sherlay retorted.

"You did not need to, my dear Sherlay. I read eagerness in your eyes and surely I discern an unfamiliar note of enthusiasm in your tone."

"You are in a mood to jest, I perceive," Lord Sherlay drawled.

Vandrington inhaled another pinch of snuff before saying gently, "I only hope I am. I should be loath to see a man whose companionship I have valued these ten years past given over to dull domesticity."

Lord Sherlay laughed. "I assure you that no such thought crossed my mind. If it had, it would not serve, since the lady gives me scant encouragement."

"But that is the greatest encouragement of all," Vandrington observed. "Now I will take my leave of you for, if I am to meet this fair unknown, I should have at least a few hours of rest. May I drive with you to Carlton House— or are your services already commandeered?"

"You may certainly come with me. I am—or rather was—going alone. Lady Chadbourne's being escorted by Sir Hugo Clavering."

"How very astute of her." Vandrington smiled, and upon this obscure remark, he left.

Sherlay's knife clattered to his plate as he stared at the space just vacated by his guest. Since he was well acquainted with the workings of that devious mind, he had no trouble in fathoming his intent. In his elliptical way, Vandrington was warning him against commitment. It was an intrusion he resented almost as much as the suggestion that he had been gammoned by Lady Chadbourne.

In the last decade, his affairs had been many but he had made no pledges. It was no mean accomplishment in a world peopled by nubile maidens, ambitious mothers, and scheming mistresses, yet, aside from his first disastrous involvement, he had not needed Vandrington's advice, nor had it been proffered. Indeed, he had often applauded Sherlay for his expertise in sidestepping the complications so often attendant upon concluding an affair of the heart. He smiled mirthlessly. That he had always been able to disentangle himself so easily was because his heart had never been touched. Indeed, more than one lady had suggested that that particular organ was missing from his body. His smile vanished. Vandrington was also aware of his attitude, so why had he felt it incumbent upon himself to scatter these little hints? It was almost as if he feared that he might be in danger of falling prey to yet another scheming woman. In that moment, he almost wished that Vandrington were still standing across from him so that he might explain that far from seeking to entrap him, Lady Chadbourne had exercised none of those wiles which other women practiced upon him. In fact, he almost wished she would—for at least it would mean she had more than a passing interest in him. The fact that she treated him with less cordiality than she did Sir Hugo Clavering galled him. Equally galling was the fact that she had the power to disturb him. Yet conversely, he was certain that if she had engaged in dalliance with him, he would already have lost interest. It was the uncertainty that intrigued him—he knew that much about himself.

Thinking about the Carlton House ball, he wondered if she would grant him any dances, and frowned. These speculations were foreign to him. Females were invariably excited when he asked for a dance, and even though she had twice refused to ride with him in the park, she had finally acceded to a third request and, judging from her demeanor, she had found his companionship much to her liking. It might please her to play fast and loose with him, but he was sure he would be able to partner her in a waltz or two. The idea of holding her slender body in his arms pleased him, mainly, he was quick to assure himself, because he imagined she would be very light on her feet, unlike Lady Emily, who moved as ponderously as the Greek statue she resembled. Lady Chadbourne was graceful in every way and so lovely . . . He gritted his teeth, not liking the direction in which his thoughts were tending. It was unlike him to devote so much time in the contemplation of any woman's charms. He turned his attention back to his breakfast but, though he had eaten very little, he summoned his man to remove it. As had happened more than once since he had arrived back from Torleigh Manor, he found himself without appetite.

Though Sir Hugo Clavering had had enough time to accustom himself to the appearance of Lady Chadbourne—having waited upon her at Chadbourne House and spent fully twenty-five minutes with her in his post-chaise as they negotiated the crowded streets which lay between Grosvenor Square and Pall Mall, he was hard put not to stare at her in the wide-eyed amazement with which he had first viewed her as she had come tripping down the winding staircase in her front hall. At that moment, she had possessed all the attributes of a vision. Indeed, in her silvery gauze-and-satin gown and with the diamond crescent in her hair, she had seemed a veritable Goddess of the Moon, depriving him of speech and rendering him unconsciously unmannerly to Miss Dalzell. He had rectified matters by kissing her withered hand—and he hoped she understood, then he forgot her completely in dreamy contemplation of the woman beside him. Even before they had alighted near the screening Ionic columns Mr. Holland had erected to shield Carlton House from the rude gaze of the throngs on Pall Mall, he was sure that none of his friends would be accompanying anyone so beautiful. Once inside the vast ballroom and seeing the incredulous glances of the men as well as the angry, appraising stares of the women, he was positive of it.

Yet, he was equally positive that the lady was completely oblivious of the excitement she was causing, mainly because she, too, was excited—but by the luxurious appointments of the huge chambers. She had commented upon them with awe as she had passed fine statuary and the wonderful paintings collected by the Regent. She had actually seemed more interested in them than in following the other glittering members of the *beau monde* into the ballroom. However, she had eventually let him guide her thither, and once inside, her little silver-shod foot was soon keeping time to the music provided by a small group of accomplished musicians.

Her hand had been resting lightly on his arm, but now it tightened on his sleeve. "I do believe that must be the Regent," she whispered.

Following her gaze, he saw the Prince at the far side of the chamber. As usual, he was resplendently garbed, his satin coat being bright green and heavy with jeweled orders. If his ex-mentor Beau Brummel had seen it, he would immediately have decried the garment as being vastly unbecoming to his bulky shape. He was, Sir Hugo thought, looking most uncomfortable and he guessed that the Prince's valet must have laced his stays too tightly. Consequently, he was amazed to hear Lady Chadbourne say admiringly, "He is a fine-looking man."

"Do you think so?" He was not altogether successful in masking his surprise.

"Oh, yes." She nodded. "His features are very good— one can quite understand why he was once known as Florizel."

Seeing the admiration in her eyes, Sir Hugo was thankful that the Regent was separated from them by a large mass of people. He was highly susceptible to flattery and he could imagine that he would be quite unmanned by sincerity, especially since he was always partial to beauty. At that moment, Sir Hugo wished he might draw his fair partner into a corner—lest she be seen and swept away from him by the Prince. He also wished that he could write his name in every empty space on the sticks of her little painted fan, but that was out of the question. She had promised him a country dance, a quadrille, and two waltzes, but no more. Jealously, he wondered what other names would be inscribed in those spaces. He knew there would be many, but the name Lord Sherlay leaped into his mind. He grimaced. Though Lady Chadbourne seemed less vulnerable to Sherlay's importuning than most females, he had twice seen her with him in the park and he was gloomily sure that the man must have been in her company more often that that. He had actually been tempted to interrogate Miss Dalzell on that subject, but he had not dared. He longed to warn Lady Chadbourne that his Lordship had a fatal fascination for women and that even the most indifferent eventually yielded to his blandishments. He had seen it happen time after time. However, he dared not voice such a caution; it would be a serious breach of manners, for though she was always pleasant to him, her attitude was that of an acquaintance rather than a friend.

While these uncomfortable reflections were passing through Sir Hugo's mind, Celia was looking about her with delight. The ballroom was as magnificent as she had always imagined it must be—and she had been quite truthful in her appraisal of the Prince Regent. Though as Lady Alys had said, he was extremely heavy, there was a compelling charm about him. He seemed to radiate goodwill. Then, it was exciting to see the beautiful gowns of the women—many of which were from Paris. She had had it in mind to wear a Paris creation herself, but on talking it over with her mantua maker and describing the gown she wanted, that astute lady had suggested that she design it herself. "For I am very sure, Milady, that there'll be nothing like it and undoubtedly you will have a great success."

It did seem as though it was being noticed—she hoped that she was not being criticized for her fancy of an underdress of white satin topped by a tunic of silvery gauze embroidered with scatterings of silver stars and a single golden moon. She wondered what he might think and felt her cheeks grow warm. It did not matter what he thought— he being Lord Sherlay, or rather, it did matter because she hoped he would find her gown arresting. She smiled. Of late, she had been aware that he was extremely puzzled by her offhand manner. She had the definite impression that she had captured his interest, but whether it was more than mere interest, she could not be sure. He did not have the vulnerability of a Sir Hugo Clavering—yet there had been moments when she had been sure he was angered and even hurt by her determined elusiveness. However, for her to savor her revenge to the utmost, it was necessary that he be at her feet, as the saying went, and then it would be time to kick him away as one did a troublesome dog.

"Lady Chadbourne . . ." Sir Hugo said tentatively, "it is the quadrille . . ."

She started and flushed. She had forgotten he was there. "Yes, of course, Sir Hugo," she murmured guiltily and accompanied him to the floor. Yet as she moved through the patterns of the dance, her mind wandered again and, as usual, it was Lord Sherlay who occupied her thoughts. Though she could not admire him, she found the game she was playing with him extremely stimulating; indeed, for the first time in ages she was facing each day with antici- pation. During her years with Gervais, there had been a dreary sameness to them. Days had turned to weeks, weeks to months, and months to years without her really being aware of time passing. She . . . she paused and stiffened. At a turn in the dance she had glimpsed Lord Sherlay across the room. He was looking very handsome in brown satin with lace at his throat and cuffs. His dark red curls were glistening with pomade and arranged à la Titus, a style which was most becoming to him—then just as she turned away again, she caught sight of a man standing near him. She had an impression of a slim, elegant figure in gray— all gray from coat to breeches to stockings to shoes. Without knowing quite why, she shivered and found Sir Hugo's eyes on her.

"Are you cold?" he asked incredulously, for the ballroom was very warm.

"No, not in the least," she assured him hastily as they were separated again.

At the end of the quadrille, she was about to accompany her partner from the floor when, of a sudden, he halted and bowing, said, "Your Royal Highness."

Turning, Celia found the Prince Regent at her side. Falling into a deep curtsey, she murmured, "Your Royal Highness."

"My dear"—the Regent's protruding blue eyes were agleam with admiration—"I have been watching you from afar and wondering why I have never seen you. Surely you have not been presented, else I must have remembered you."

"No, Sire," she breathed, feeling as if her heart had suddenly leaped to her throat.

"Sire, this is Lady Chadbourne," Sir Hugo said dutifully.

"Oh, you are the widow of Lord Chadbourne, who was my father's friend. That explains why I have not seen you. He was long away from court."

"Yes, Sire, he was very ill in the last years of his life."

"I know that and am sorry for it. So you have been in mourning?"

"Yes, Sire."

"But are now out of it and will, I hope, do me the honor of dancing the next waltz with me."

She drew a deep quavering breath. "The . . . the honor is mine, Sire."

"No, no, no, Beauty must always reign supreme." He had taken her hand in his hot grasp and he held it tightly. "Yes, Beauty must be Queen or"—and there was a touch of dryness to his tone—"ought to be."

Seeing the bitter twist to his mouth, she guessed that he was thinking of his hated wife, the Princess Caroline, and having no good opinion of the lady, she gave him a warmly sympathetic smile. She was rewarded by an answering smile and a hurtful squeeze of her fingers. Then he was whirling her about the floor in time to one of the popular German waltz tunes. In spite of his bulk, he moved gracefully, but he looked very warm and he was breathing hard. Also, she found his hard stare disconcerting. It seemed to her that he was actually speaking with his eyes, but if he were trying to send a message, its content eluded her. Then, as the music ended, he smiled. "That was exhilarating." He was actually panting now. "But it is passing hot in here—too many candles, too many fires. Should you care for a breath of air, my dear?"

Mindful that she had promised the next waltz to Sir Hugo, she was uncertain of what to answer. One did not, she thought, refuse the request of a Prince. "I . . . if you . . . yes," she blurted, feeling very gauche.

"Good, very good, yes, very good." Putting his hand firmly beneath her arm, he led her from the room.

Since she was looking at him, Celia did not see—but she did feel—a battery of eyes upon them. Then they were through the doors and down a corridor and through yet another set of portals, all obsequiously opened by handsome young men in powdered wigs and the magnificent livery of the Royal household. Though she could think of no reason for it, she felt extremely edgy, a sensation that increased as they came into the garden. She had a vague impression of clipped hedges and patterned beds, illumined by lights cunningly concealed in the foliage. It was very lovely, but it was cold and, involuntarily, she shivered.

"Ah, we should have fetched your cloak," murmured the Regent, slipping his arm around her shoulders and drawing her close to him. "Do you feel warmer now?"

"I . . . yes," she stammered. The Prince was still panting, or was he merely breathing deeply? She was not sure. She was beginning to feel very uncomfortable—because that arm on her shoulders was heavy and his hand was beginning to casually caress her breast, a liberty which she would not have hesitated to dismiss with a slap, but one could not strike the Regent.

"The night is kind to you, my dear." He smiled. "And I can see the moon reflected in your eyes . . . two little golden moons to match that which is emblazoned on your gown."

"You are k-kind to s-say so, S-Sire." Involuntarily, she stepped backward.

"Am I frightening you?" he questioned. "You must not be frightened." He was moving closer and now he was putting his other arm around her.

"Lady Chadbourne!" A cool voice reached her from some distance away. "Our dance . . ."

The Regent had tensed and, dropping his arms, he stepped away from her as out of the darkness emerged the tall, slender man in gray she had seen with Lord Sherlay. His eyes were full of surprise. "A thousand pardons, Sire. I did not dream that you were here." He frowned. "I was told only that Lady Chadbourne had gone into the garden. Obviously my informant was having a little jest at my expense. I will see to it that his laughter is soon quelled."

"No . . . no reason for that, Vandrington." The Regent sounded extremely discomfited. "I'd not have any . . . unpleasantness. You were to dance with this charming lady?"

"I believe you will find my name written on her fan," he said audaciously, "but if your Royal Highness has the prior claim . . ."

"Oh, no, no, no, I am very sorry, my dear fellow. I had no notion, none at all . . . Please claim your partner and promise that you'll take no reprisals."

"I am not one who takes such matters lightly, but . . . very well, Sire, since you wish it, I shall not proceed any further with the matter."

"Good, very good." The Regent smiled at Celia. "It was delightful, my dear. I thank you for the waltz . . ."

"It was an honor, Sire," she said.

"Ah, yes, just so . . . well, good evening, my dear." Moving more hastily than she would have imagined his girth would allow, he vanished among the shrubbery.

The man on whom she must look as her rescuer turned to her and in the light from the little lamps on the trees she saw that his eyes, which were as gray as his garments, were brimming with laughter. "I hope I was not *de trop*."

"Oh, no," she breathed thankfully, "I was quite at a loss. I . . . I mean . . ."

"I am sure you were." He nodded. "That is why I followed you. Might I hope that you will favor me with that dance? It woud be, I think, politic."

"I should be delighted, sir," she said gratefully.

"And I, too, must confess myself delighted. I might add, my dear Lady Chadbourne, that the Regent as always, has shown excellent taste."

"You are very kind, sir. You have the advantage of me, however, since I do not know your name."

"Vandrington . . . Sir Charles Vandrington," he said.

Her rescuer was a fine dancer—light on his feet and supremely graceful. Yet despite her gratitude for his timely intervention in the garden, there was something about him that she could not like. She tried to tell herself that it was his odd mode of dress, but it was more than that—it was also the way he looked at her, almost as if he were trying to see through her. She could only be pleased when the music finally ended and he escorted her from the floor. She was immediately surrounded by numerous gentlemen, all begging the privilege of a dance, and then she saw Lord Sherlay moving purposefully toward her. At that moment and in her confused state of mind, he took on the guise of an oasis in a desert of strangers. It had not been part of her strategy to dance with him immediately, but she could not think of that—she could only acquiese as he masterfully demanded the next waltz.

She should have guessed, she thought, that their steps would suit. He too, was a fine dancer and for the duration of the waltz she felt singularly at ease and oddly safe, which was very odd considering her partner's identity, but comparing him with the intimidating Sir Charles Vandrington and the importunate Prince he actually seemed the least of three evils. Indeed, she hardly noticed that he was leading her toward the edge of the dance floor until they were there, and moving through the masses of guests into the hall, she found herself in a small dark alcove, near a long window. Through it she could see the large golden moon which the Regent had so elliptically praised.

She stared at Lord Sherlay dazedly. "Why have you brought me here?"

He did not answer. There was an angry yet ardent look in his eyes. Putting his arms around her, he strained her against him fiercely, holding her so tightly she could not move, could not avoid the long kiss he pressed on her lips, and for one single moment she did not want to avoid it. Then reason returned and with it an all-consuming anger. She struggled furiously until he finally released her.

"H-How dare you?" she cried, thrusting her hand against her mouth as if she would wipe his kiss away.

Fury flared in his eyes, too, then it vanished as he said coldly, "Then . . . you save your favors only for princes?"

"On the contrary," she retorted freezingly, "my favors are only for those whom I love and respect!" Swiftly she left him, running back through the darkness until she saw the lights from the ballroom streaming across the floor. Waiting only a moment until she regained her composure, she stepped back inside, standing against the wall.

"Lady Chadbourne, I have been looking everywhere for you." Sir Hugo joined her hastily. He added with a tinge of reproach. "This was our dance and . . ."

"Sir Hugo," she interrupted, "you must take me home."

"My dear Lady Chadbourne." Concern leaped into his eyes. "What can be amiss?"

"I . . . I have the headache. I must go. At once."

He looked distressed and disappointed, but he bowed. "Of course," he said politely. "If that is what you wish, I shall call for my post-chaise immediately."

Miss Dalzell, who always found it difficult to sleep, was playing solitaire in the drawing room when she heard the voice of Ames, the butler, in the hall, followed by that of

Celia. Glancing at the clock on the mantel, she was astounded to find that it was only a few moments past twelve—far too early for her to have returned from the ball. Coming into the hall, she came to a dead stop, putting a trembling hand to her heart, for Celia, her face white and her eyes blazing, was standing by the stairs.

"My dear, whatever is the matter?" quavered Miss Dalzell.

"Oh, Cousin Laura," Celia cried. "I am glad that you are yet about, but you must retire for the night, for we'll need to be astir early and on our way."

"On our way?" repeated Miss Dalzell blankly.

"We are returning to Chadbourne Hall," Celia rasped.

"To . . . to Chadbourne Hall . . . returning . . ." Miss Dalzell regarded her in amazement. Then, as if that announcement were not startling enough, Celia, usually so calm and serene, burst into wild sobs and rushed up the stairs as if the very devil were after her!

6

THEY HAD LEFT the Purple Unicorn, an inn on the Great
North Road, early that morning, changed horses at noon,
and now in the late afternoon they were within a few miles
of Haltwhistle and Chadbourne Hall. Eschewing the heavy,
lumbering traveling coach, Celia had ordered the lighter
post-chaise and such luggage as there was had been strapped
on top. That she had not taken the traveling coach and a
second coach for their effects attested to the fact that Lady
Chadbourne was not settled in her mind as to whether or
not they would winter at the Hall. Miss Dalzell, clinging
to a strap, and Rose, seated across from her, looked at each
other from time to time but neither had any comment to
make—Rose, because it was not her place to question the
whims of the Quality, however much she resented being
whisked back to the North, when she had been looking
forward to a meeting with the footman she had met at
Torleigh. He had returned to London and called upon her
just as he had promised, and she was much put out not to
be seeing him. She had left numerous messages with the

kitchen staff and could only hope that they would be delivered—though certainly she was not quiet in her mind about it, there being that pert, forward little kitchen maid, Betsy, who did not seem to know her place and flirted with any gentleman who came near her. To think of her made Rose expel a hissing breath and grit her teeth.

Miss Dalzell did not resent their hasty departure. She was disturbed because she could see that Celia was upset, though fortunately, she had calmed down since her surprising outburst of the night before last. In fact, she seemed her usual serene self, which was a relief, for in five the years since Miss Dalzell had come to live at the Hall— brought out of kindness when her elderly, spendthrift father had died, leaving her quite alone in the world and all his income gone on the horse races and cockfights that had occupied his days—Celia, only twenty-one when she had arrived, had been so calm and capable, and the way she had cared for poor dear Second-Cousin-by-Marriage Gervais she might have been twice her age. Laura Dalzell had a sigh for the late Earl; he had doted on Celia and she had seemed very fond of him, despite the very great disparity in their ages. When she had heard of the marriage, she had been quite shocked to think of Gervais taking a seventeen-year-old girl, with no dowry, as his wife. Her father had been equally shocked, predicting that the filly would lead him a merry dance, but of course it had not happened, and to have seen Celia looking so distraught when she had returned from Carlton House pained her. She wondered if the young man who had escorted her had had anything to do with her troubled state of mind, but she doubted it. Something else must have occurred. She knew she ought not to be curious and certainly she would never pry—but she could not help but wonder about it, for even though the storm had passed, Celia was not herself. Ever so often her face would darken and Miss Dalzell was positive that she was still dwelling on whatever it was that had taken place.

She sighed and clutched the strap tighter. Though it did

not much matter where she was as long as she had the
security of a roof over her head, she had looked forward
to a season in London. Chadbourne Hall was so big and
so gloomy in the long days of winter. Already there was
a penetrating chill in the air; she could feel it, even through
the heavy woolen shawl that she had wound around her
fleece-lined cloak. She could only hope that Celia would
change her mind and bring them back before the roads
became too mired.

Celia, staring out on a lonely stretch of moors darkening
under a setting sun that was leaving in its wake gray clouds
edged at their extremities with bands of pink, was inordinately pleased to see the barren landscape. They were within
a few miles of the Hall and the nearer they came, the calmer
she felt. Once inside, she would be able to regain the peace
and serenity she had enjoyed during the last few years. She
was unused to the tumultuous angers that had stirred her
since the night of the ball and which increased in intensity
each time she thought of Lord Sherlay. That he had dared
to act with such an abysmal lack of propriety, clutching her
in his arms as if she had been some passing maidservant!

She had thought better of him—yes, despite her rancor,
she had believed him to be a gentleman. Then, to treat her
in such a manner and to suggest that she entertained am-
bitions to be the mistress of the Prince—he had not exactly
said that, but that was what he might have implied! To
think of those moments was to become angry all over
again—at him and at herself, because for a moment, she
had remained passive in that hard embrace. No, unfortunately, she had not been entirely passive—for one moment,
she had actually yielded, with parted lips, to the pressure
of that seeking mouth. It had not been a minute, it had only
been a second and she had been caught off-guard, surprised . . . but it was useless to think of reasons or of excitement or . . . She only knew that by his actions, her plans
had been utterly ruined. There could be no question of
leading him on, of tantalizing him—he had been too pre-

cipitate and she had responded in kind, striking him across the face. If she had been clever, she would have dismissed his caress lightly—teased him, cajoled him, and avoided him—then, he would have continued to pursue her. As it was, she had not only revealed her very deep dislike of him in those hastily uttered words, she had proved herself shocked by his want of conduct. If he were to wait on her again, she could not consent to see him—or could she? There was no use dwelling on that most regrettable incident. She put her hands up to her face and found it burning and hated him the more! Early on in their marriage, she and Gervais had been in Cornwall and she remembered walking along the seashore after a tempest—the little waves crossed and crisscrossed each other as if they had lost all sense of direction. It seemed to her that her emotions must resemble those moiling waters.

Finally, they had reached the long semicircle of a drive that brought them to the portals of the Hall. Celia, staring out the window, was suddenly reminded and daunted by a vision from the past. She saw her younger self, ill and listless, staring apathetically from the window of another post-chaise and being further depressed by the lineaments of the mansion, square against a bleak and darkening sky. It had seemed so lonely amidst the masses of ancient trees that rose above it. Since that time she had come to love its storied chambers and to appreciate the changes which had taken place since its rebulding two hundred years earlier. Now, again, she was minded of its loneliness and how skeletal the trees would look once they were entirely denuded of their yellowing leaves.

Another unwelcome memory arose, and she saw Gervais lying in the immense fourposter of the master chamber. How small and shrunken he had looked, his mouth caved in, his eyes dimming, while outside, gusts of wind-driven rain had spattered against the windows with a force that had made the panes rattle. She had been holding his hands and they were so cold—so cold and thin, she could feel the bones beneath the dry, aged flesh. Yet, at the last those hands had feebly closed on her fingers and pulled, as if in dying he had wanted to take her with him into his waiting tomb.

She shuddered, wishing she had not acted on impulse—she did not want to be back at Chadbourne where such memories lurked, but the chaise had halted, and the door was being opened. Slowly, reluctantly, she alighted and as she walked in the direction of the heavy oaken door, scored with the marks of pikes wielded by a group of insurgent Presbyterians who were angered by the Chadbournes endowing an Anglican church in a nearby village, all thoughts of peace were blotted from her mind. She had the disturbing impression that she had willfully condemned herself to prison. She threw a wild glance over her shoulder at the chaise, wishing she might command her coachman to turn once more toward London, but there was no turning back. Lord Sherlay barred the way.

A dense mist rolled around the house, bringing with it a dampness that invaded the rooms, rendering every space not reached by the heat that issued from the fireplaces dank and miserable. Celia, wearing an old woolen gown, had chosen to remain in the library. It was her fifth day at Chadbourne but it felt more like the same number of weeks. Standing at the window, she stared into an empty grayness that blotted out everything, giving her the impression that all the surrounding land had been obliterated, leaving them stranded nowhere. Moodily, she turned away, gazing at the tall shelves that lined three walls and branched into additional shelving in the middle of the vast chamber. More of the unwelcome memories that had been pouring into her mind during the past week arose, and again she was confronted with her younger self, no longer the miserable sixteen-year-old, sobbing herself to sleep in the small chamber she occupied in the Dower House, but turned seventeen and, amazingly, the bride of the Earl of Chadbourne, wedded to him the previous day in the ancient chapel which was a part of the original Hall.

It was the morning after her wedding—after that confusing night when she had discovered what it meant to be a married lady. The Earl had been very gentle—at least at first, and gently apologetic at the last, when she had cried out at the pain. She had been apologetic, too, because she feared she had distressed and disappointed him. Later, she had gratefully gone to sleep in his arms. Yet, in the morning, she had been in an odd, shy mood, thinking of the night, and she had fled to the library, where she had always found solace in reading. She had tried to read then, but it had been impossible. She had been unable to rid her mind of what had transpired in the night. Despite his gentleness, he had invaded her, claiming for himself the secret, inmost parts of her body, which no one had ever seen or touched before. It had been frightening—she had wanted to run away. She could laugh at her naiveté now—but no, she did not want to laugh, because in a sense, it had happened again. Some deep part of her had been touched and disturbed but, unlike her wedding night, unlike all the nights when she had submitted patiently to the Earl's demands, she felt oddly stirred and restless. She had never felt that way before. No, that was not true. Long, long ago, Ceci Gramont, lifting her lips for her first kiss, had experienced precisely those same stirrings.

She stamped her foot in a fury because it had been he, Lord Sherlay, who had pressed that kiss upon her lips—her willing, wanting lips, but the man he had become should not have had the power to excite her anew—not when she hated him as much as she did!

Turning to a shelf, she took out a book. It was a leather-covered volume, its surface unpleasantly clammy from the damp. Taking it to the fireplace, she held it toward the blaze until it dried, then moving back to a sofa a few feet away, she sank down and opened it at random. Then her eyes widened in consternation as she read:

> Yet send me back my heart and eyes,
> That I may know and see thy lies,
> And may laugh and joy, when thou . . .

Slamming the cover down, she tossed the book to the floor, glaring at it. To have picked a work of John Donne's, to have opened it on those verses once recited to her by Armin Sherlay that day in the cathedral, seemed more than a coincidence —it was almost as if he were haunting her!

She stared down at the fallen book, then, conscience-stricken, picked it up. It was no way to treat one of Gervais' volumes. He had loved to read and many of the books in the library had been purchased by him. They came from all over the world, and locked away in one cabinet were such rare treasures as a Gutenberg Bible and a First Folio of Shakespeare. There were other treasures in that library— a portfolio of Hogarth sketches, a Claude Lorrain landscape, a Rubens Venus, a bronze shield which had been found in Kent and which dated back to the Roman occupation, a collection of fine Japanese porcelain figures and some exquisite Meissen figurines. To look at them was to remember Gervais detailing the history of each. She wished he could be with her—she needed his protective presence, then she shook her head; she did not want to think of him either. Moving to the sofa, she sat down and stared into the flames and presently, feeling her lids grow heavy, she was glad to yield to that encroaching sleep. It would keep her from thinking.

"Celia . . ." A hand was on her shoulder, gently shaking her into wakefulness.

Opening her eyes, she found the room much darker and the fire only a mass of glowing embers. Miss Dalzell stood beside her, smiling timorously. "What o'clock is it?" Celia demanded.

"Close on five, my dear. I should have looked for you here . . . I cannot think why I did not. I do hope I did the right thing but Mrs. Blake and I did search for you . . . Why I did not guess that you were in the library, I do not know, save that I was so confounded by the accident. Since I did recognize him, I felt there was nothing else I could do, poor gentleman—and the horse. I am very much afraid that it must be destroyed, though he was not much injured and for that I am grateful. He could have broken a collarbone or his shoulder. Of course, he has been considerably shaken up and his ankle hurt—I should not be surprised if he were very stiff and sore tomorrow. I have put him in the dressing room of the Red Chamber, it being so much smaller and cosier and he so chilled, poor young man. William has lighted a fire and he is seeing to his garments which, of course, are very much muddied. I had William give him one of poor Gervais' nightshirts."

It having been impossible to interrupt Miss Dalzell in midnarrative, Celia had listened in growing mystification until her companion, finally ceasing to speak, looked at her apologetically. "I do not understand. Who is this gentleman?"

"He came looking for you, dear, and was lost in the mist, which was very thick and is now a pelting rain. He is staying at the Green Goose and the landlord, Mr. Briggs, you know, gave him your direction, but the mist closed in and his horse stepped into a hole and he was thrown. As I explained, he is not badly hurt, only a little dazed. Fortunately, he was able to find his way here. I do not know what might have happened had he wandered onto the moors."

"Cousin Laura, dear, what is his name?" Celia asked patiently.

"Oh, my, that is it. I did recognize his face—he has been to see you more than once, my dear, but he was so exhausted. He was distressed over the horse, too, which he had hired at the inn. He seemed so very sorry for the poor animal and then he fainted . . ."

"Fainted!"

"He recovered almost immediately—burnt feathers, you know, then William gave him brandy, but I did not get his name. It seemed expedient to bring him up to a room as quickly as Griselda could get it readied. You will no doubt know who he is, poor young man. Most likely Rose would have known, too, but Mrs. Blake said she'd slipped away to see her mother—very naughty of her."

"She did not 'slip away,'" Celia corrected. "I gave her permission to visit her mother for a few days. But would this gentleman be Sir Hugo Clavering?"

"Sir Hugo Clavering? Perhaps, I am not sure. He dropped right off to sleep, William told me. I hope you do not mind that I gave him that nightshirt that belonged to Gervais?"

"No, of course not, but I do wish you had learned his identity, Cousin Laura."

"Well, I expect you could come along and see him, my dear. I do not think you would awaken him. Actually, now that I think on it—I believe it must be Sir Hugo."

"It sounds very much like something he would do. He is not very wise." Celia grimaced.

"Young men in his . . . er, condition seldom are," Miss Dalzell commented archly.

"He should not be in that condition," Celia pointed out coldly. "To have come all this way . . . it's outside of enough! I have never given him the slightest encouragement!"

"In my young days, and I cannot think the world has changed overmuch since then, love-smitten young gentlemen did not need much encouragement to act . . . very foolishly. I can remember . . ." Miss Dalzell broke off hastily and sighed, looking pensive. "But that is of no consequence. Shall you look in on him, my dear?"

"No." Celia shook her head. "I'll not disturb him, poor

Sir Hugo—let him sleep. The horse is in the stables?"

"Yes . . . unfortunate beast."

"Are you certain that it must be shot?"

"I fear so. Of course, I do not have Papa's knowledge of horses, but it was on three legs and the fourth looked broken."

"I think I shall examine it."

"But, my dear . . . the rain."

"No matter, I want Joseph to look at it, too. He has a great knowledge of bones. I am sure Sir Hugo would want me to do what I can since you say he was so distressed over it."

"Yes, I was quite impressed. He seemed far more concerned about the animal than himself . . ."

"That is kind in him," Celia commented approvingly. "I did not know he had such a side to his nature. I will fetch my cloak."

As she hurried from the room, Miss Dalzell, looking after her, heaved a sentimental sigh. The idea of a gentleman coming all the way from London just to see Celia showed a very romantic nature. She wished that dear Celia had been a bit more appreciative. She had actually seemed more annoyed than flattered. It seemed a pity, considering his accident, but actually fate might have favored him after all, for it was certainly raining very hard, and from the looks of that lowering sky, there was very little chance of its clearing for at least a day—maybe even longer—and, after that, the roads would be sadly mired. Expected or not, Sir Hugo would need to remain at the Hall for several more days. There was no telling what could happen in that time!

Despite her avowed design not to remarry, Celia was too young and too lovely to remain a widow. She ought to wed again and Sir Hugo was a handsome man—and the fact that he had left the inn, despite the weather, showed that he was persevering as well as ardent. Celia might be very happy with him. She sighed again. It was easy enough to be alone when you were young, but when you grew older it was a different matter. She was thinking of Jeffrey Drane, who had courted her once—such a pleasant young gentleman, but Papa had discouraged him as he had discouraged all the others. It had not mattered about the others—but dearest Jeffrey, and Papa being so horrid to him. She had wept for days; she blinked back her tears. It was silly to cry over something that had happened fully thirty years earlier, and Jeffrey married to sweet Anne Pettingill and the father of two lovely sons and three pretty daughters—probably the lot of them married and with children of their own, by now. She moved to the window and stood staring into the darkness—a wind was moaning about the corners of the house. She shivered and then she smiled—it promised to be a real storm!

As Miss Dalzell had said, the horse's leg was broken and Joseph's only office could be to destroy it, which he had promised to do—once he had received Sir Hugo's sanction. That fact, together with the suffering look she had seen in the eyes of the animal when the groom had shone his lantern into its stall, had depressed Celia. She awakened the next morning with the same sense of gloom. Her mood was not lightened by the sight of huge rivulets of water coursing down the window panes. Thinking of Sir Hugo, she shook her head. It would be impossible for him to ride back to the inn and the idea of spending more than a few hours in his company did not appeal to her—not in the least!

Though he was charming and always well informed as to the latest *on dit*, she did not share his pleasure in town scandals—nor did she care to hear about Mills, cockfights, or which horse was the current favorite at Newmarket or Ascot. Yet, if such topics wearied her—how much more tiresome were the compliments, invariably accompanied by either soulful or reproachful looks. Though usually she managed to laugh these away, it would be very difficult to keep laughing for upwards of two to three days, especially when he had sustained injuries which had been inadvertently incurred on her behalf—though the Good Lord knew she would have been the last to have encouraged him in this great piece of folly!

It was, she was well aware, unkind and ungrateful of her, but she did hope that his probable stiffness and soreness would keep him abed that morning. She would give her servants instructions to bring his breakfast to him and that would postpone the evil hour when she must undertake the burden of being his hostess. She glanced out the window at that water-soaked landscape and again she bitterly regretted the impulse that had driven her to Chadbourne Hall, an impulse for which she did not scruple to blame Lord Sherlay's unprovoked actions!

The old French clock that stood on the sculptured marble mantelpiece in the center of the Long Gallery tinged and Celia smiled. Then guiltily she smoothed the expression away. It was half past the hour of eleven and evidently Sir Hugo was still abed. May, sent to look in on him at nine, had reported that he was still sleeping and Celia had accordingly sent him a note telling him that he might rest as long as he liked. She had added that she would be in the Long Gallery until noon did he wish to join her—but, as yet, he had not availed himself of that invitation, suggesting that her craven hopes had been fulfilled and she spared the necessity of dealing with his inanities and his apologies, poor boy.

The more she thought about it, the more surprising it seemed that Sir Hugo would come all this distance to see her. Certainly, she had never encouraged him that much, but Cousin Laura had insisted that love-stricken gentlemen did not need encouragement. It must be true. Celia sighed. It had been a long time since she had been faced with such a dilemma. Then, with a slight shock, she realized that she had never been faced with it. She had been wed at seventeen and she had been out of mourning only a short time. Once more she would have given much to have had her husband with her. She had not realized the difficulties attendant upon being a single woman, and a wealthy one, at that. She smiled derisively.

There was a possibilty that Sir Hugo had been attracted by the reputed size of her fortune. She wondered what he might say were he to learn that that same fortune had been left her in a way that made it impossible for a prospective bridegroom to claim it. Early in her marriage, Gervais anticipating a time when she might be left a widow and subject to the attentions of fortune hunters, had appointed trustees instructed to abide by her direction alone. She smiled and then sighed, looking toward his portraits, though actually his features adorned many of the paintings that lined those brocaded walls, there being a great family resemblance throughout the Chadbourne generations.

She recalled her feelings of awe when, attended by her brother as well as the Earl of Chadbourne, she had been first shown through the Long Gallery with its scarlet and gold decor and its ceiling painted to represent Apollo's journey through the heavens. She had never been in so vast a chamber and though she had still been lost in melancholy, the sight of those paintings had momentarily lifted her spirits. While some of them were no more than passable—others had been done by Holbein, Van Dyke, and incredulously, a seventeenth-century Chadbourne had been depicted in the dark, gold-shot oils that she had learned to associate with Rembrandt. She had been informed that it was indeed a Rembrandt, painted when the Earl's great-grandfather had fled the Roundheads to spend years of exile in Holland. His son had been painted by Lely and the Earl's immediate family had had the benefit of portraits by Romney and Gainsborough—the latter having executed the likenesses of the Earl and his bride, Lady Drusilla. In those days she had little dreamed that her own portrait, done shortly after her marriage, by James Ward, a young member of the Royal Academy, would also grace those scarlet walls.

Glancing at it now, she frowned—she had never liked

it; the artist had made much of the white streak that marked
her hair, painting it wider than it actually was. Furthermore,
she had been in a good mood when she had sat for him—
but she had emerged as pale and melancholy while the
muslin gown she had worn had also undergone a transition—
it looked like wisps of gauze. However, the Earl had pronounced himself much pleased with it. Close beside it was
her favorite painting—done in 1766 by one Domenico Cav-
allero, a traveling Italian artist. It depicted Gervais as he
had been at nineteen.

Though she had been told that the artist was not famous,
obviously he had been a man of no mean talent, for the
young face beneath the powdered wig had been filled with
vitality—to look into his glowing dark eyes was to want to
know him. Indeed, in the early years of her marriage, she
had often surreptitiously scanned the Earl's features in hopes
of finding some trace of that vibrant youth. Impulsively,
she rose and moved across the room to the portrait. She
regarded it ruefully. Possibly she had been a little in love
with it for, often when she was lying beside her husband
at night, she had tried to imagine that it was that young man
who was cradling her in his arms—his hazel-green eyes not
hazel green. He had brown eyes, brown, brown, *brown,*
she reminded herself fiercely. Then she tensed, for she had
felt a draught of cold air and turning found that the door
had opened. Sir Hugo had decided to join her after all. As
she started forward, he appeared on the threshold, but it
was not Sir Hugo who limped inside. It was Lord Sherlay!

Coming to a dead stop, she stared at him incredulously.
"You!" she whispered.

He sketched a bow and winced as he straightened up.
"The same," he answered dryly. "I gathered from your . . .
er . . . missive that you believed me to be Sir Hugo Clavering. I am sorry to disappoint you—though I must say I
am at a loss as to know how this particular misunderstanding
occurred?"

"I . . . C-Cousin Laura . . . uh, Miss Dalzell, she did

not have your name and I . . . or rather she thought . . ."
She looked at him confusedly. "But why are you here?"

"If you will permit me to sit down, I shall explain. I am
not quite myself, yet."

"Oh, yes . . . your accident." Looking at him, she saw
that he was very pale and that he was swaying slightly. She
was at his side in an instant, putting a sustaining arm around
his waist. "Come . . . you must sit down near the fire. It's
chilly in here. I do not know why you are from your bed."

"You need not help me, Lady Chadbourne. I am able to
walk . . ."

Ignoring his protest, she kept her arm about him until
they had reached the chair that was nearest the fire. "Sit
here," she ordered sternly.

With a slight twitch of his lips, he obeyed. "I thank you,"
he muttered. "It was not my intention to appear before you
in such straits . . ."

"Should you like some brandy?" she asked.

"No, I am quite all right, though I am grateful for the
fire." He gazed about him, saying with another slight smile,
"All your buried ancestors?"

"My husband's," she corrected. "I fear the injuries you
suffered . . ."

"No injuries," he interrupted almost angrily. "I am only
stiff . . . as you must have been when you fell on the hunting
field."

"No, I . . ." she began and remembered that she had used
her nonexistent pains as an excuse to avoid *him*. "I do not
think I was hurt quite as badly. I fell on leaves . . ." She
frowned. "The horse . . ."

"The horse," he interrupted again, his brows contracting,
"is there a chance . . . ?"

"No," she said regretfully. "Joseph and I had a look at
it last night. I hoped he might be able to bind its leg—were
it a mere sprain. Joseph's our second groom and he has
great knowledge of horses. He has cared for all our sick and
lame animals. He said it was best that this one be destroyed.

He would do it, but I thought we must wait for your permission."

He winced. "You have it, of course. Poor beast. I hold myself accountable. I should have known better than to chance the ride."

It was on the tip of her tongue to agree, but glancing at his stricken face, the words would not come. "I expect you are not familiar with our Northern fogs."

"No," he said. "I've spent little time in these regions. My father had a hunting box in Scotland, but I am not much on the sport. My own estate's in Sussex."

"Oh, where?" she asked interestedly, and was on the point of telling him that her nurse's sister's house was close to Ashdown Forest, where she had often gone. Fortunately, she remembered just in time that she had claimed never to have left the North as a child.

"It's near Worthing," he said.

"Oh, yes, I have been in that district. The weather is certainly more felicitous."

"Much. Our rains seem gentler and the countryside's more cultivated. Yet there's a certain wild beauty to the North country."

"There is," she agreed, "and the moors are lovely in the spring and summer when the heather, the harebells, and the pinks are in bloom."

"Are you a nature enthusiast, then?" he asked curiously.

"Oh, yes, I am fond of nature in all its aspects."

"Even the rain?"

She could not restrain a smile. "I was thinking more of flowers and plants—though the rain is necessary for them, I expect."

"I expect so," he agreed. He was silent a moment, then with an obvious effort, he said, "I imagine you must wonder why I have come?"

His query gave her a slight shock as she realized they had strayed very far away from the point, actually falling into a casual conversation when the circumstances attendant

upon his presence were far from casual, especially when
viewed in the context of their last disastrous meeting. "Yes."
She nodded. "Why did you come?"

"I..." He paused, for at that moment Miss Dalzell,
looking concerned, came in, crossing quickly to his side.

"Oh, my dear Sir Hugo," she said anxiously, "William
told me you were up. He said you'd insisted on coming
down when you'd have been much better off in bed. Putting
your boots over that ankle! That was most unwise."

Celia looked down at his boots—they fitted tightly to his
legs and she noticed for the first time that his clothes were
much the worse for wear—with a rent in his jacket and mud
stains on his breeches. "Your ankle," she said concernedly,
"did you sprain it?"

He looked annoyed. "It is nothing."

"But it is," Miss Dalzell contradicted. "William said that
it is badly twisted."

"Blast William," he began explosively. Then, evidently
trying to control his temper, he added, "You must excuse
me, but surely I am the best judge of my capacities."

"I should think not." Miss Dalzell's tone was actually
motherly. "Else you would have worn the slippers William
offered you."

"Yes, that's true," Celia agreed.

"He needs more rest," Miss Dalzell stated.

"I tell you I do not." He rose swiftly and took a quick
turn around the room. "You see I am—quite able to—to..."
He suddenly clutched at the back of a chair.

"Oh, dear." Miss Dalzell fluttered to his side and pushed
the chair behind him. "Do sit down."

He remained standing. "I am no child. I have been a
soldier."

"Yes, so you said," Celia returned. "But when soldiers
are injured, they, too, take to their beds. Cousin Laura, I
suggest you fetch William."

"Yes, dear, at once...it is quite the best thing." She
hurried out of the room.

"Please sit down," Celia said.

Though he obeyed reluctantly, he leaned against the back of the chair with obvious relief. "I feel like an old woman," he complained crossly.

"An old woman would have had more sense than to come down that long flight of stairs in the hall," she retorted. "It must have been an agony if your ankle is as bad as Cousin Laura seems to believe it is. It is also a long walk to the Gallery. Why did you not remain in your chamber?"

"Because I had your note."

"Which suggested you remain where you were."

"It suggested that Sir Hugo Clavering remain where he was, and I realized that I was here under false pretenses."

"You could have righted such misapprehensions with a mere message."

"I felt it was better to explain in person. And I have not yet explained to my satisfaction or, I fear, to yours..."

"You must not tax yourself..."

"Lady Chadbourne," he burst out. "I assure you 'tis far more taxing to remain silent. I beg you will heed me. At our last meeting, I behaved unpardonably—in word and action. I regretted both immediately and came the next day to beg your forgiveness but you had gone, and I cannot but think that it might have been I who was responsible for that hasty departure. I felt it incumbent upon myself to seek you out..."

"And you traveled all these leagues because of that?" she asked incredulously.

"Because of that, yes, and when I saw your face as I entered this chamber, I knew myself to be right. Lady Chadbourne, my reputation is not... of the best, but I would not have you believe me a complete rogue when I... I do hold you in such high esteem—whatever my actions of the other night."

She regarded him amazedly. His manner had changed completely. He was no longer either suave or controlled, and the drawl she had believed habitual was gone from his voice. He looked earnest, apologetic, and somehow more youthful. For a moment, time rolled back and she saw once more the vulnerable young man of the cathedral—facing her equally vulnerable self. Then the never-to-be-forgotten-or-forgiven cry of "Harlot!" was loud in her ears and she was recoiling from the cruel blow which had broken her heart and shattered her life.

That Lord Sherlay had not apologized to Ceci Gramont— but Lady Chadbourne was a different matter. She was of his world and consequently, she merited his respect and— she thought—something more. He would not have come such a long distance merely to apologize. With a surge of triumph, she realized that inadvertently her retreat had been a clever bit of strategy. It behooved her to make the most of it this time and since he would be her guest for at least a week—or perhaps longer—she would have all the opportunity she needed. She said soothingly, "I assure you, my Lord, there were business matters called me home and . . ." She paused as Miss Dalzell, accompanied by a tall, grave-faced young footman, hurried in. "But here is William."

He continued to regard her. "Listen to me . . ." he urged.

"Later, my Lord," she told him firmly. William will help you up to your chamber and I think it would be best if you took laudanum and slept for the rest of the day. Possibly, too, Joseph should bind your ankle."

He had a weak smile for that. "The horse doctor?"

"My husband was not above consulting him when it came to broken or sprained limbs. I'd send for the doctor, but the rain . . ."

He raised a protesting hand. "Enough, I was but teasing. I'll be most grateful for Joseph's ministrations. But tell me, have I your forgiveness?"

She hesitated, then she said slowly, "Yes, you do have it, my Lord."

"You are more than kind," he replied in a low voice. "I . . ."

"Please," she interrupted. "You must let William help you to your chamber."

"I do not think I need help," he said rising quickly. "I am . . ." A curious surprised look came over his face and then he fell back on the chair in a faint.

"Armin!" Celia whispered, kneeling beside him. "Oh, Armin . . ." She was on the point of tears but then swiftly collecting herself, she cried, "William, come here."

Miss Dalzell darted forward. "Oh, dear," she mourned. "He is a most impulsive and headstrong young man. It was dreadfully unwise of him to come down. You should have insisted that he remain in his bed, William."

"I did not think it my place," the footman replied, looking anxiously at Lord Sherlay.

"But . . ." Miss Dalzell began.

"You know he is right, Cousin Laura," Celia interposed. Her momentary distress had vanished. She added calmly, "I believe it is as well that he swooned."

"Celia, dear, so unfeeling," Miss Dalzell protested.

"On the contrary," she retorted. "If he had not, he might still be protesting at being helped. As you say—he is very headstrong. I hope he'll not be too heavy for you to lift, William. We could ask Matt or . . ."

"No, Milady, it is not necessary." Bending down, William lifted Lord Sherlay with surprising ease.

"Good," Celia approved. "I suggest you take him to the Blue Chamber. I'll have Mrs. Blake send one of the maids to build a fire and make up the bed. Being larger, it will be more comfortable for him."

"Of course, I should have thought of that. He is tall," Miss Dalzell said. "Oh, dear, poor Sir Hugo . . . so ill-advised."

"He is not Sir Hugo," Celia contradicted as William bore him from the room. "That is Lord Sherlay."

"Gracious!" Miss Dalzell explained. "How surprising!"

"Quite," Celia commented with a twisted smile.

7

LORD SHERLAY STRAIGHTENED his tumbled covers. He had just awakened and still in his mind were the bits and pieces of dreams which had threaded through his sleeping brain, whirling into oblivion during his brief periods of wakefulness. He knew it was the laudanum, a drug he had not taken since the agony brought on by the shoulder wound which had invalided him home from Portugal His fall had made that same shoulder ache almost intolerably and there were other assorted pains. He had not believed himself so stiff and sore until he had committed the folly of going down the winding staircase and losing himself in the chilly State Rooms of this vast and gloomy mansion.

It was, he thought, a very strange setting for Lady Chadbourne. Though it had been her home during her marriage, she did not belong in it. He thought of Briarton Abbey equally large but much more to his liking. Its windows looked out on the rolling downs of Sussex while beyond the trees that surrounded the Hall stretched the barren moors, which despite Lady Chadbourne's defense of them, did not appeal to him. He felt a surge of longing for the Abbey. Yet, he had not spent much time there of late, even though it had once been his ambition to settle down, oversee

his lands, and raise a family, thus flouting the curse of
Abbot John. In a sense, he reasoned, he had flouted it. He
had not fared "badly"; he had had a very good time and,
at thirty, he had already outlived his father by two years.
To think of that heedless young peer was to remember his
mother, dead these three years past. He did not like to think
of her—she had been very disappointed at the abrupt change
in the plans he had often discussed with her before he had
turned twenty. Yet, typically, she had never questioned him
on it. However, it had been his own guilts which had kept
him from visiting her as much as he would have before . . . He
frowned, trying to banish those fruitless recriminations. If
he were not confined to this confounded bed—he glared at
it and then laughed. He ought not to visit his wrath upon
that unoffending piece of furniture. Actually, it was very
beautiful with its richly carved headboard and its high can-
opy, suggesting that it had been fashioned a hundred years
earlier.

He glanced around the chamber—the blue velvet hang-
ings on the bed matched the draperies at the long, rain-
washed windows. The walls were hung with a blue damask
and a fine old Chinese carpet lay on the floor. The furniture
was Chippendale, though one of the cabinets was inlaid
with ivory and looked to be from Italy. It had been very
gracious of her to put him in such felicitous surroundings.
It was more than he deserved, he thought, and was surprised. The compunctions which had visited him since that
night at the ball were new to him. It was foreign to his
imperious nature to feel humble and in the wrong. Ordinarily he would have resented anyone who had roused such
sentiments; he had, he knew, resented his mother for that
very reason, but he did not resent Lady Chadbourne. Celia.
He pictured her in his mind and realized that she had figured
in most of his dreams.

He remembered their encounter in the Long Gallery. It,
too, was a beautiful chamber, but he had not liked it. All
those portraits had oppressed him. He had, he now remem-

bered, dreamed about them, too—an odd, ugly vision about
the lot of them stepping down from the walls to surround
her, closing her away from him—and most prominent
among them had been one which he had guessed to be her
husband, still claiming her from his grave. Lady Alys had
told him that he had been very old—Emily, too, had stressed
that. He wondered why she had wed him. Nine years ago,
she must have been no more than seventeen. Though such
marriages were common enough among the *ton*, he did not
like to think of Celia Chadbourne wasting her vibrant youth
upon a man who might have been her grandfather. Surely,
there must have been other, younger men who had coveted
her. If only he could have been one of them—if only he
could have met her instead of Ceci Gramont, but in those
days, Celia Chadbourne was probably dreaming on her sequestered little island.

He stared at the drops of water coursing down the window pane, and as he looked at them he seemed to see a
face mirrored in the glass—Ceci Gramont, laughing tender
eyes staring up at him—had she been so tiny, or was he
seeing her as even smaller than she was? He was no longer
sure. He did remember her huge blue eyes and those long
lashes. Celia Chadbourne had blue eyes but they were darker
than those of Ceci, and her lashes were even longer. Her
hair was similarly dark—he wondered how she had come
by that white lock and guessed it was a birthmark. His
thoughts drifted back to Ceci—he wondered what had happened to that lovely child. At least, she had seemed lovely.
She had seemed so many things. A line of Donne went
through his head and he chuckled dryly, remembering that
he had actually quoted it to her.

> Yet send me back my heart and eyes,
>   That I might know and see thy lies . . .

Odd that it had been so singularly apt. She must have
been struck by that, but being as clever at mummery as her

sister, she had managed not to betray herself. She had never betrayed herself, not once. Innocence had been reflected in every glance, smile, and action. Her impersonation had been perfect—even to the stricken look in her eyes that last night, which had been the night of the second day he had seen her—the last day, the terrible day of disillusionment. Forty-eight hours out of a lifetime, and yet he still thought on them and hated her—hated her and that Abbess, who had acted the role of chaperon as cleverly as she had impersonated similar ladies on the boards. Vandrington had seen her in various of those parts.

He wondered how many other men had been gulled by the pair of them and touched his arm. There was a slight indentation on it, where Madreston's bullet had grazed him. One of his mistresses had commented that it looked like a birthmark and he had said, "Yes, that is what it is, my dear—a mark signifying the birth of Wisdom—coming forth instantaneously like Minerva from Jove's cranium." She had not understood—nor had she understood when, clutching her to him, he had made violent, hurtful love to her, so that she had moaned in pain. He had been remorseful and gentler—soothing her, but never telling her that for the moment, he had seen superimposed upon her fair features, the face of Ceci Gramont, who had killed all tenderness in him and made him immune to love—or so he had believed. He did not believe that anymore—the heart which he had thought to be as cold as that of Vandrington had grown warm again. There was no sense deluding himself—he was in love with Lady Chadbourne!

He grimaced, remembering Vandrington's suggestions that she was leading him on—he realized that those seeds of suspicion had taken root in his mind. That was the reason he had drawn her into the alcove and his embrace. For a second, it had seemed to him that she had responded, but, he thought, that must be in his imagination or, perhaps, wishful thinking. Then, the next day, Vandrington had detailed his interference with the Prince's plans to seduce her.

In common with Lord Sherlay, he had seen his Royal Highness lead her into the garden. His description of her obvious fear as the Prince closed in for the kill had made him feel worse than ever about the accusations he had leveled at her that night. He was glad to have had Vandrington's explanation but he was also puzzled, wondering what had prompted him to rescue the lady.

"It was my chivalrous instinct," Vandrington had averred.

Sherlay did not believe that. It was more likely his bent for mischief which had driven him to interrupt what might have been a most disastrous *tête-a-tête*—unless he, himself, had been attracted to her. He could not believe that Vandrington's views on females had not changed in all the years he had known him. He was aware, too, that they had done much to shape his own thoughts and actions. After his disastrous experience with Ceci Gramont, Vandrington's cynicism had come easily to him and it had served him well, helping him to avoid wedlock, a condition he, in common with his mentor, had abhorred—but not anymore. The dull domesticity at which Vandrington shuddered and sneered would not be dull with Lady Chadbourne beside him.

She was so different from the other women he had met— so unspoiled. He could imagine her presiding over the Abbey. He could never have envisioned any of the other women he had known in the house his mother had graced. Yet, through his reprehensible conduct, he might have lost her. Feeling an odd moisture in his eyes, he raised a hand to rub them and found that his cheeks were wet. Unbeknownst to himself, he had actually been weeping. Feeling shocked and mortified at such weakness, he hastily wiped his tears away. Uneasily he wondered what Vandrington might have thought had he found him in so lachrymose a condition—and over a female! Then, he realized that for once he did not care what Vandrington might think. Furthermore, he was mightily relieved that his erstwhile companion was not present to puncture his new-found hopes with a few telling darts from his venom-coated tongue.

"Is it true, dear Lord Sherlay, that his Majesty once shook hands with a tree in the castle park?" Miss Dalzell asked. The lady was in her element that afternoon. Seated near Lord Sherlay's bed, she talked at him much, a listening Celia thought, like Coleridge's Ancient Mariner with the hapless Wedding Guest. Fixing him with a compelling if not a beady eye, she had been nattering on about the madness of the King ever since they had come to visit him.

It was a topic which had interested dear Papa very much, she had explained. Papa had been presented to his muddled Majesty many years earlier and had found him dull but certainly sane—so naturally when rumors began to fly, he had been eager to learn as much as he could. However, living in the remote village of Whenby, one had great difficulty sifting the true from the false. Papa, of course, had known many affluent Whigs in his young years in London, but their letters were full of such strange tales regarding the King's condition that she had sometimes wondered if they had not been prevaricating.

Celia, her head bent over her embroidery, bit down a smile that threatened to betray a naughty amusement. Unlike Cousin Laura, she was aware that his Lordship was being sorely tried by the ordeal of listening to her and endeavoring not to betray his annoyance or, she guessed, frustration. Having preceded Cousin Laura into his bedchamber, she had seen the eagerness in his eyes when he had greeted her. She could almost feel sorry for the subsequent diminuation of that enthusiasm as Miss Dalzell glided in behind her, inquiring as to the state of his health and hardly allowing time for an answer before she rushed to the next question, which she was doing even now.

"At one time, his Majesty was reported to believe that

London was under water and he able to sail his yacht over Westminster Abbey . . . surely that cannot be true, my Lord?"

"His delusions have been many, ma'am," replied his Lordship a little desperately.

"Yes, I do know that. I have wondered if some did not spring from his disappointment in love. They say Lady Sarah Lennox was quite beautiful and though dear Queen Charlotte is imbued with a great many virtues, I cannot but think her appearance must have proved a little off-putting to His Majesty, for all they had fifteen children." She blushed. "Oh, dear, I fear I have been indelicate. I expect you must know the Queen, do you not?"

"I have been presented to her—but I cannot say that I know her, ma'am."

"Then—there is the purple dressing gown."

"The purple dressing gown!" Celia could not forbear questioning. "What might that have to do with Queen Charlotte, Cousin Laura?"

"Oh, I was not referring to her, my dear. I was but following a train of thought. They say that the King's hair and beard have grown very long and that he wanders about the corridors of the palace in a purple dressing gown. Does he?"

"Er . . . I believe so, ma'am." Lord Sherlay appeared to be having some trouble controlling a twitching of his lips.

"And imagines he is talking with angels?"

"Angels and his grandfather, yes." Lord Sherlay's tone was smothered.

"Oh, isn't it a pity? Papa, at the end had all his wits about him—though he was cross. The gout, you understand. However, I am pleased that he was cross rather than mad— such a burden for the poor Queen and I am sure, too, that it must be quite distracting for his sons—what does the Regent have to say about it?"

"Nothing to me, ma'am."

"But certainly he must be greatly concerned."

"I think," Celia interrupted, "that it is time Lord Sherlay rested. He looks weary."

"Oh, are you?" Miss Dalzell fastened her gaze on Lord Sherlay's face. "I pray I have not tired you. It is just that it is so seldom that I have ever met anyone connected so closely with the Regent—though Papa was on good terms with Lord Sheffield, he passed through Whenby only once and, of course, I dared not question him. Papa would have thought it very forward of me." She rose. "You are looking better, though. According to Joseph, you have suffered only a mild sprain. Though I expect the rain cannot help. I have always noticed that the finger I broke aches more in the rain. Indeed, it aches when there is about to be a rain. Papa used to call it a regular weather vane. I do not know if that happens with a sprain, though . . ."

"We will leave you, now," Celia said. "Come Cousin . . ."

"Yes, dear. Good afternoon, my Lord." Miss Dalzell gave him a warm smile and hurried from the room.

"Lady Chadbourne," Lord Sherlay said hastily as Celia seemed about to follow her. "Could you not remain a moment? There is something I should like to ask you."

She paused by the bedpost. "Yes, my Lord?"

"You . . . could you not stay with me a little longer? I've not seen you this whole day nor talked with you."

She gazed at him out of wide, surprised eyes. "But you know I cannot remain here alone. It would not only be lacking in propriety, but my household staff must hear of it and the news spread through the whole county."

He moved restlessly. "I am hardly in a position to do you any harm," he said gruffly.

"As Cousin Laura has said, you have suffered no more than a mild sprain—and though I am sure you'd not infringe upon my hospitality, it is necessary that we avoid the appearance of evil. However, if you are bored, may I not send William up to you with some books?"

There was a gleam in his eyes and she noted that they

looked more green than hazel. "Were our situations reversed and you at my mercy, Lady Chadbourne, I should not treat you so ill. But enough! I shall accept the books though I must call them, at best, a poor substitute."

"Have you any literary preferences, my Lord?"

"I will hope that I may depend on your tastes, Lady Chadbourne."

"I shall try to please you."

"You do so without trying."

She sketched a slight curtsey. "You are kind, my Lord."

"I refute the accusation. I am honest. And though you may not believe it, I have other virtues as well, which given the opportunity, I would demonstrate. If you were to remain alone in here, you'd take no more harm from me. I hope you believe that."

"I do believe you, but again, I fear my cousin must wonder why I am tarrying so long. I pray you will excuse me. I will go and select your books. You will have them shortly. Though I think you must rest as well as read." With a conciliating smile, she added, "I bid you good afternoon."

"It would be a better afternoon—if you would stay."

She smiled again and, raising her hand in a little salute, she hurried from the room. On reaching the library, she sank down on the chair behind the desk and rested her chin on her cupped hands. Her heart was pounding—she was also feeling both hot and cold, almost as if she had fallen victim to a sudden fever. It was a reaction she did not hesitate to lay at Lord Sherlay's door. It had been an ordeal remaining in his company and being required to subdue her still-active hostility. Yet, all in all, she could not be dissatisfied as to the progress she was making.

Clearly, he was not used to dealing with females impervious to his charms. It was undoubtedly a new experience; she guessed that by his puzzled frown and chancy looks at her as Miss Dalzell had been questioning him about the King. She could guess that he had been most disheartened by the time she had left him. She fully intended to improve upon this initial success. In a sense, she was already experiencing some little measure of revenge and, as Shakespeare had said, its taste was sweet—sweet enough to whet her appetite for more—and as she thought about it, her eyes brightened. She had suddenly conceived an entirely different way of getting even with him—he wanted her company, did he? Well, he might have it. It would be a harsher punishment than she had originally contemplated and it might put certain restraints upon herself. However, that did not matter—what mattered was that he would suffer as much as Ceci Gramont had suffered. He was a proud man, she knew, and he would live to see that vaunted pride in shreds and himself worsted by a mere woman.

She moved to the shelves. Fortunately, she knew that he had a taste for poetry. It was one that Gervais had shared. She chose Scott's *Marmion* and *Lady of the Lake*, Byron's First Canto of *Childe Harold*, and Milton's *Paradise Lost*. She resisted the temptation of including the poems of John Donne.

It was late and Celia, roused from slumber, stared around her darkened chamber. She did not know what had awakened her but immediately her eyes were open, she was fully conscious and her mind full of the thoughts that had been plaguing it when she had fallen asleep. Sitting up in bed, she clutched her knees and stared out windows unstreaked by rain, unmisted by fog. The shrunken moon was yet a clear white—as bright in its way as the sun that had been shining all the previous day. The clarity of that sky presaged another bright day and the end of Lord Sherlay's week-long sojourn beneath the roof of Chadbourne Hall. He had been up for three days. His ankle was much improved but his temper was not, for Celia had continued to use her companion as a buffer between them. Necessarily, Miss Dalzell took her meals with them and she had also remained in the library where he and Celia had played cards. Though she had had the good sense to hold her busy tongue during play, her habit of hovering near the table had proved distracting to Lord Sherlay—which might have been why he continued to lose. Shortly before they had finished playing that night, he had said disgustedly, "I begin to believe either in your luck or my lack of it." Judging by the long look which had accompanied that statement, she knew that his implication was embracing more than a mere card game.

She wondered if she had not been too discouraging to him. During dinner, it had seemed to her that he had spoken with some relief about returning to the inn. She had meant to allow him a few moments of her time after they had finished the card game. Cousin Laura usually went to bed immediately after they laid down their cards, but tonight she had lingered on, babbling about the Chadbourne Luck and Celia's own luck in having it when it often skipped whole generations.

Celia had endeavored to stem the flow by saying with a laugh, "Come, I cannot believe that Lord Sherlay wishes to hear more about the Luck." She had even dared to add, "It is late. Are you not weary, Cousin Laura?"

"No, no, not in the least, my dear," that lady had hastened to say, "though you are kind to ask. Now I think it particularly interesting that Gervais' great-uncle Andrew had the Luck as a small boy but when he grew older—he lost it." She had detailed the sorrows of Andrew and then gone into the fluctuating fortunes of other Chadbournes. She had still been speaking when Lord Sherlay, rising suddenly, had said with something less than his usual courtesy, "If you will excuse me, ma'am, I find I have a headache and must retire." Without waiting for her answer, and favoring Celia with the smallest of bows, he had added, "Your servant, Lady Chadbourne," and left the room in what seemed three strides.

"Well"—Cousin Laura had cast an affronted glare after his retreating figure,—"I must say I thought him excessively unmannerly."

"I expect he is not feeling quite the thing," Celia had

answered—her own head throbbing from the effects of conversation which had battered against her like so many pellets of hail, with the one difference that hail storms generally ceased quickly. Indeed, she had never found Cousin Laura's maundering quite so . . . she suddenly tensed.

She had heard something. The floor was creaking. It often creaked at night—there were rustlings in the walls, too. She suspected mice in the wainscoting—but this noise was different. It sounded like footsteps! She peered into the darkness, but she could see nothing. Then she gasped, for the moon-cast shadows of the windows that lay along the floor had been disturbed by another shadow—that of a man in a long robe such as Gervais had been wont to wear over his nightshirt. The idea of ghosts flitted through her mind and out again instantly. Floors did not creak under the measured footsteps of the dead—nor was it a ghost who said on a note of relief, "Ah, you are awake. I must speak to you."

Celia gasped. "Lord Sherlay . . . how dare you come in here?" Her voice rose. "Get out or—or I shall summon . . ."

He moved quickly around the bed, and catching her in one arm, he sank down behind her, holding her against him in a viselike grip, while he slipped his free hand over her mouth. "Hear me," he commanded in a fierce whisper. She struggled against that hard grasp but to no avail. "Hear me," he repeated, "and I shall release you. As I told you, you'll take no harm from me, but I will speak to you."

She shook her head, still struggling, and when he lifted his hand for a second, she started to cry out only to have the sound instantly muffled by the replacing of his hand.

"Celia." His voice was actually stern. "I understand well enough what liberties I am taking, but I begin to think we will never be alone. Tonight I was close to carrying that blasted woman bodily from the room, but of course, that would have served me nothing and there is something I must say to you. Though you've given me scant encouragement, I . . . love you. I did not ever think I could meet a woman whom I could both respect and love as much as I do you. I want you for my wife. You need not give me an answer right away, but I pray you'll not scorn the method of my wooing nor dismiss me immediately, please." He removed his hand.

Her pulses were pounding. She was breathless. "You are . . . are m-making m-me an offer?" she stuttered.

"Yes, an offer, and I do apologize for the way in which I have couched it, but this past week I have been driven mad, being with you and never being able to tell you what is in my heart. Since the first moment I saw you—at Torleigh Manor, I have thought of you night and day. Indeed, I have had the odd fancy that we may have met in another lifetime. I know you will laugh at this illusion, but no matter . . . Oh, Celia, I do love you so very much."

She heard desperation in his voice, and pressed against him as she was, she could feel the heavy beat of his heart. It seemed very loud in her ear. "I . . . hardly know what to . . . to say." She imbued her tone with a quotient of distraction.

"I have told you . . . say nothing, yet. I may be a fool, but in spite of the way you have avoided me this past week . . ."

"I have not avoided you, my Lord," she interrupted, "but as I told you, it was necessary to consider the proprieties."

"Well, you have considered them," he said dryly. He rose and stood by the bed, adding uncertainly, "I have felt that you are not entirely indifferent to me or . . . am I wrong?"

She had never imagined that Lord Sherlay—or at least the Lord Sherlay she had known in the past weeks—could have sounded so ardent and so unsure of himself. There was a youthful cadence to his voice, and unwillingly she was once more reminded of the youth in the cathedral, but she could not think of him, that boy, who had told of his love for Ceci Gramont and treated her so shabbily afterward—never giving her a chance to explain and then forgetting her very existence! She said, "*No*, you are not wrong, my Lord, I am not indifferent to you." It was no more than the truth—for hatred was certainly not indifference.

"Then . . . dare I hope . . .?"

"As you have said, I must think on it. I never dreamed . . ."

"I know. I do understand, dear Celia, but I . . . I should like an answer soon."

"I . . . I had planned not to marry again . . ."

"But plans change. I shall take comfort in the fact that you've not given me an out-and-out refusal. As you know, I am leaving tomorrow morning, but I shall remain at the Green Goose for two days. Do you believe that in that time you . . . you might possibly reach a decision?"

"I . . . you do me a great honor, my Lord," she remembered she ought to say.

"Never mind your proper phrases," he rasped. "Will you let me hear from you before I return to London?"

"I will see . . . but p-please, I beg you will leave me now . . ."

"I shall, and again forgive me that I invaded your . . . sanctuary. I am aware that my conduct was reprehensible, but had I not been desperate. I assure you I should never have resorted to such measures. Now . . . my dear love, I shall bid you good night."

"Goodnight, then," she whispered. He moved swiftly from the room and as she heard the door close she thrust a pillow against her mouth to choke down her laughter. She had won! And she could bless her dearest Cousin Laura for having added the *coup de grâce* that had brought him hotfooted to her side! Cousin Laura coupled with her own indifference, of course. That had been a favorite ploy of her sister Bella's, she remembered. Borrowing another page from Bella's book, she would keep him dangling as her sister had her Bostonian merchant—possibly even as long

as two days—then, as he was ready to leave, she would
send William with the message and, in due time, she would
be Lady Sherlay!

She slipped from bed and moving to her dressing table,
she opened her jewel box, staring at its contents, illumined
by the thin moonlight. At last she would have the opportunity to return a gift . . .

Thinking about it, she laughed again, and then suddenly
she began to weep and sobbing returned to her bed, huddling
down beneath her covers and pressing her face into the
pillows. She hardly knew why she was weeping—possibly,
it was not she at all but little Ceci Gramont, who was about
to have her dearest wish fulfilled—nameless Ceci Gramont,
who, due to the careful planning of Celia Chadbourne,
would soon be twice-named and well named. Lady Alys
had once told her that Lord Sherlay was exceedingly proud
of his family and with reason, since a Sherlay had fought
beside William the Conqueror while another member of the
clan had ridden with Richard the Lion-Hearted on the Cru-
sades and still another had watched his brother King John
sign the Magna Carta. There had been a Sherlay who had
died at Agincourt and a later Sherlay had dared to champion
Sir Thomas More and he, too, had died, but other Sherlays
had lived and prospered and certainly they did not court
harlots or marry bastards. She tried to produce another
mocking laugh, but the tears still flowed, persisting through
the long hours while the moon waned and the stars paled.
She finally fell into a fitful slumber.

8

THE CIRCULAR DRAWING room of the Dunglass Mansion on Portman Square was ablaze with lights from a magnificent Venetian-glass chandelier. More lights in sconces affixed to pale green walls shone down on banks of flowers—including rare orchids and other hothouse blooms. It was here that the supper celebrating the wedding of Lord and Lady Sherlay had been held.

Lord Dunglass, Marquis of Bly, was a dear friend of the late Lord Chadbourne and had known his young wife since the day of her marriage. He had insisted on standing up with her in lieu of a father. His lady, in turn, had provided what the numerous illustrious guests, following the lead of the Prince Regent, had termed a magnificent repast. His Royal Highness, having dutifully toasted the bride and groom, had gone his way with many of his entourage, but as many others remained to drink to the happiness of the couple.

However, one guest, Lady Alys Torleigh had, much to the surprise of her husband, hastily left the chamber, a wisp of cambric clapped to her eyes. He followed her and, catching her by the wrist just outside the door, whispered, "It is customary for females to weep at weddings, though I do not know why since the lot of you scheme hard enough to be brides..."

He received an indignant glare. "R-Rolf," she protested. "You offered for me and..."

"I am not talking about you," he was quick to assure her, "but as I was saying, though it's customary to weep at weddings, it's been my understanding that the subsequent festivities are supposed to be a happy occasion. Yet you've been looking damned blue-deviled all this evening. Lord, one might think you were at a funeral."

"Shhhh." She put a trembling finger to her lips and quickly moved to another door. Opening it, she peeped inside and then beckoned to him.

Following her, he found himself in a small drawing room. Fortunately, it was unoccupied and to insure that it might remain that way, he closed the door and stood against it. "Now...what's amiss?"

"I—I did not know I looked so cast-down. I have been smiling until my lips are stiff."

"And so they look—stiff. Fortunately, I do not believe anyone noticed save myself—but I repeat, what is the matter with you?"

Lady Alys saw a chair close to where she was standing and sank down on it as if her legs would no longer hold her. "It...it's Celia." She raised woeful eyes to her husband. "Rolf, I am so afraid for her."

"Afraid?" he responded incredulously. "Why—when she has made the match of the season and snared one whom I thought to be a confirmed bachelor?"

"Do not say 'snared,'" she begged. "It was he who did the pursuing. I have it from Miss Dalzell that he hunted her all the way to Chadbourne Hall."

"And there held a knife to her throat until she consented to wed him?" her husband retorted with heavy irony.

"I cannot believe she did it of her own free will," Lady
Alys said. "It is all a great puzzle. If you'd seen her as I
did, when she was dressing for the ceremony...she was
in a dreadful taking, pale and trembling. She very nearly
cried off."

"And did not your mama tell me that you were in a
similar distraught condition?"

"It was not like that."

"She managed to speak her responses loud and clear."

"I heard desperation in her tone."

"Nonsense, it's your imagination."

"It is not," she said indignantly. "I know that it is not.
I cannot help but feel that this is all folly and three parts
our fault."

"Ours?"

"Yours, rather. I did not want to invite him to Torleigh,
but you insisted." Lady Alys arose and moved restlessly
around the room.

Following, he caught her by the hand, bringing her to
a halt. "That is the most arrant nonsense I ever heard.
Sherlay's a very good fellow, and despite your croakings
I've reason to believe the pair of them'll do very well together. He's a changed man since he came back from the
North—and you must admit he looked very happy at the
ceremony."

"Why should he not? Celia's beautiful, rich, and..."

"And I do not understand why you are in the fidgets,
Alys. Let us go back and toast them." Taking her arm, he
led her out of the drawing room and back into the dining
room.

As they stepped inside, Sir Charles Vandrington, clad
in his usual gray, translated for the occasion into satin and
silk, was standing against the wall staring moodily at the
bridal pair. A second later, he was sauntering toward them.
"So he's here after all," Lady Alys murmured.

"I didn't think he'd get back in time," her husband said.
"He's been in France."

"Does he never doff that eternal gray?" she asked.

"Tonight he seems to have the temper to match it," Lord Rolf commented.

"He did not look very pleased," she agreed. "I wonder why."

"I am sure he thought Sherlay, in common with himself, was a confirmed misogamist. Indeed, I have often thought that to be the basis of their friendship—for certainly they are not very like."

"I disagree. I think they are very similar. Both equally lacking in heart."

"Not true," Lord Rolf retorted. "Sherlay has a heart even if he don't wear it on his sleeve, and I vow it's in full view of us all."

Vandrington, meanwhile, had stopped beside Lady Emily Hammond, who with her husband, stood a short distance apart from those who thronged about the newly married couple. Seeing Vandrington approach, she paled perceptibly, but meeting his saturnine gaze, she forced a smile. Pinching her husband's arm, she said, "Here's Sir Charles, Hammond."

"Oh." Lord Hammond, a tall, burly man with a plain countenance lit by large, short-sighted blue eyes, looked vaguely at Vandrington. "Evenin', Sir Charles . . . Devil of a crush."

"Quite," Vandrington replied, his eyes lingering on Lady Emily.

"I did not see you in church, Sir Charles," she remarked.

"Mainly because I knew nothing of the festivities until I returned to my lodgings and found Lord Dunglass' invitation."

"You were not informed about the marriage?" Lady Emily asked in some surprise.

"Alas, I have been in France of late."

"Lovely, ain't she?" Lord Hammond surveyed the bride through his quizzing glass. "New to the town . . . expect that accounts for Sherlay's success."

Lady Emily tensed. "I should say rather that it was her success, my dear, coming from nowhere to marry a Sherlay."

"She's a Chadbourne, Emily," Lord Hammond reproved. "That's hardly nowhere."

"A Chadbourne by marriage," Lady Emily emphasized. "An orphan with none to give her away save a friend of her late *husband's* family."

"Maiden name was Grayce . . . nothin' wrong with that family."

"I cannot think of any branch of the Grayce's that lives in the North—at least none that *I* know," she said coldly.

"You have a vast acquaintance, m'dear, but I cannot believe it embraces all England."

"Celia Grayce," mused Vandrington, fixing his cold gaze on the bride. "There's a look about her that reminds me of someone I once knew."

"Who?" Lady Emily asked abruptly.

He shook his head. "I am not sure. It was a fleeting impression and has fled. But I must offer my felicitations to the . . . er . . . happy pair." He bowed. "Your servant, Milady . . . my Lord."

Celia, standing beside Lord Sherlay, felt curiously detached, almost as if she were hovering over that brilliant assemblage, looking down on the young woman in the ice-blue satin gown, a diamond and sapphire tiara set in her dark hair—with the white lock much in evidence, an effect she had demanded from Rose, who had, until that instruction, been making an effort to bury it beneath her dark curls.

How strangely the maid had looked at her when she had said, "No, it must be seen—even though none save myself appreciates its significance." Yet, even as that command had left her lips, she had been seized with a strange terror, and that had been the emotion glimpsed by Lady Alys, who had entered her chamber at that moment.

A memory of something Bella had once said flashed into her mind. It had been in answer to a question the young

Ceci had put to her, "Are you never afraid when you go out on stage?"

"Always." Her sister had given a mock shudder. "When I am waiting in the wings for my cue, I wish myself a million miles distant—on a ship bound for anywhere. Then," Bella had said with a giggle, "the curtain rises and I am fine—and know that I belong exactly where I am."

She, too, wished herself a million miles away and she could not think she belonged at the side of the man to whom she had just been wed. If only she had never left Chadbourne Hall—if only Gervais had not died. When he was alive, she had been peaceful. She was envious of that other self. Since she had met Lord Sherlay again, she had not known a moment's peace. She could compare herself to a field upon which opposing armies fought and clashed—the sound of their strife was in her ears, and beneath their trampling feet her flowering plants and her sweet grasses were crushed— only devastation remained. No, that was no proper analogy—the strife was in her own head and the devastation would be of her own creating.

She pressed a hand to her bosom and felt the object— the *talisman* that dangled on the end of a fine gold chain. She had removed it from her jewel box the previous night, and when Rose had gone from the room, she had slipped it beneath her heavy diamond and sapphire necklace. No one knew it was there—but before the night had ended, the man at her side would know and the triumphant smile would be wiped from his face.

Her detachment was fading. She was aware of him again—he was wearing a green velvet coat and a diamond pin glittered in the fall of lace at his throat; his waistcoat was white satin as were his breeches. Fine white silk stockings and black patent-leather shoes completed his attire. His dark red hair was carefully arranged. She had never seen him look quite so happy. If it were not for the object on the chain, she might have been sorry for him, but to touch it was to remember a conversation with her sister. Bella had come into her bedroom and sat down on the bed, where for two days, Ceci had lain, staring at the ceiling, unable to eat, unable to sleep, unable to weep because she had cried all her tears away as over and over she envisioned and was still envisioning that moment when Lord Sherlay had struck and denounced her.

"Child." Bella's voice had quivered with indignation. "I am loathe to speak to you on this matter, but you have been sent a letter which I have seen fit to open—since it comes from *him*."

"Him?" Ceci had whispered. She had felt a surge of hope that died immediately she remembered her sister's tone.

"Yes—and I think you must let me read it to you. I would spare you this pain—but it concerns a decision you must make. Will you listen?"

"Yes."

In a cold voice, Bella had begun. "'Miss Gramont: in my ignorance as to your nature, character, and intent, I parted with an heirloom of great worth to me. I am not speaking in monetary terms but rather of its significance and antiquity. It came into our family in the year 1530— and was a present from Sir Thomas More to one of my ancestors. It has always been worn by the eldest son. When I gave it to you, I intended only that you should keep it until I might replace it with a betrothal ring. Under the circumstances, I should like its return and herewith enclose three hundred pounds which is considerably more than its value— if you were, as you no doubt intend, to sell it. I believe this sum will compensate you for its loss. I enclose my direction and hope to have it in my possession on the morrow. Sherlay.'"

That letter, ashes these ten years, had been burned into her memory—the money had been returned the same day, enclosed in a packet which had contained no accompanying explanation. Thinking on it now, she stared down at her left hand. On the third finger was a wide gold band and above it his diamond betrothal ring.

"Ah, my dear Lady Sherlay, might I offer my very good wishes for your . . . happiness?"

She glanced up quickly, startled by the mode of address, which still sounded strange and unfamiliar to her ears, though she had heard it all that evening. Looking into pale gray eyes, under gun-metal gray eyebrows, she was startled at the sudden chill which went through her. However, she managed to quell the threatening shiver and said with a smile, "Sir Charles Vandrington."

"The same, Lady Sherlay." The gray glance shifted to Lord Sherlay's face. "My dear Armin, I left you a bachelor and return to find you a benedict."

Celia, listening to the exchange, felt a tension in Lord Sherlay's arm. She noted that his eyes had turned watchful but his smile remained. "That is no more than the truth, Vandrington. I hope I may share in your good wishes."

"But I thought they must be implicit," Vandrington returned. "Though I am surprised. Other than Lady Dunglass' invitation, I found no other word awaiting me at my lodgings."

"I had believed you in France, and had I your direction, you would have heard from me there."

"How remiss of me not to leave it." Vandrington sighed. "But no matter—again let me give you my felicitations and wish you both as much happiness as you deserve."

As he bowed and turned away, Celia barely restrained another shiver—she had found his glance peculiarly intent, and meeting it, she had experienced an odd flicker of memory—she had seen that expression before. She tried to tell herself that it was when he had rescued her from the unwelcome attentions of the Regent, but that was not true. She had seen him somewhere before that—though where or when, she could not recall—nor could she dwell on it, for Lord Sherlay was speaking to her and there was urgency in his tone.

"It grows late, my love, and it's time we were away, do you not agree?"

Looking up and meeting his ardent gaze, a pulse in her throat began to throb. She longed to beg that he take her back to her own house—but that was impossible. A tenant had been found for it, but that was not the reason they were not going to it. She was wed to him and they would spend the night at his home, then, on the morrow, he planned to take her to Briarton Abbey, but she could not think of the morrow . . . Between the morrow and the night . . . But he was waiting for her answer. "Yes, let us go, Armin."

She glimpsed uncertainty in his eyes—as if he had been surprised by her hesitation, but at her response, he smiled at her tenderly. "I do believe you are a little afraid of me, my dear love. There's no need to be afraid, I promise you."

"I am not afraid," she replied in a low voice, realizing that of all the lies she had told him that day, this was possibly the greatest. Quite suddenly, she was terrified. It took all her courage to keep her hand on his arm as they moved toward the door, stopping only to thank their host and hostess and to receive further salutations from the guests. Then they were in the hall and he was wrapping her fur-lined cloak about her and escorting her to the waiting carriage.

"A million miles . . ." she murmured as he climbed in beside her.

"What did you say, my dearest love?"

"Nothing, my own," she replied between stiff lips and then could say nothing more as he, gathering her into his arms, kissed her gently and then—not gently at all.

Winding her arms around his neck, she forced herself to respond because, after all, that was part of her plan. She was relieved to discover that it was not as unpleasant as she had feared.

Ignoring the footman who opened the carriage door, Lord Sherlay carried his bride into a hall softly lighted by a center chandelier which cast myriads of beams, rainbow-colored from the prismed drops, upon the paneled walls. Another servant, an elderly butler, had come forward and addressed

Lord Sherlay, who had in turn answered and identified him as Bellows. She acknowledged the introduction but she did not actually see him because her husband was still holding her in his arms, cradling her against his chest gently, as one might carry a child.

She did not look at him, though she was aware of his eyes on her. Her own glance was for the curve of the staircase, for the carved balustrade, and then on the number of closed doors in the upstairs hall. Once they had reached the second floor, she saw that there were paintings—they caught the light, but she could discern only a blurred mass of color. Her heart was pounding; there was a constriction in her throat, which she knew to be fear. She had imagined the scene which was about to take place, all that day, all that week, all that month. She had dreamed about it at night— envisioned it unfolding up to a point, and that point the end of her revelation. She could not go beyond that—could not determine his reaction or, with a little shudder, was aware that she was afraid to determine it.

A strain of melody ran through her mind. She had no trouble identifying it. At Gervais' request, she had played it for him on the harpsichord. It was excerpted from an opera, which had not yet been heard in London—Mozart's *Don Giovanni*. She recalled its subtitle, *il dissoluto punita*— the dissolute punished. It was particularly fitting that she should remember it at this moment. Sherlay had been dissolute and in common with Don Giovanni, whose exploits he had emulated, he was about to be punished. Again in common with Don Giovanni, he would be sent into a Hell of his own creating—but would he take her with him? Unlike the stone statue of the Commendatore, who had come to fetch him, she was made of more perishable stuff. He could easily throttle her, but he would not, for she had provided herself with protection in the form of a small but deadly pistol, heavy in the silken reticule that hung from her wrist. Its weight gave her confidence.

There was softness beneath her. She was startled and

looked up at him in amazement. The softness was a huge bed, its silken coverlet drawn back and its fine sheets and soft blankets exposed. While she had been pondering her revenge, he had carried her into a large chamber, lit by candelabrum on the dressing table and on the mantelshelf and also by a fire glowing on the hearth. Those flames were reflected in his eyes, which were brilliant yet tender. The absurd thought that, from what she had read of the libretto, Don Giovanni was never tender, arose and was lost in some dark pit where most of her thoughts were falling. His caressing hand was on her hair; it moved lightly to the swell of her breasts—then he stepped back, whispering, "I shall leave you for the nonce and send Rose to you."

Rose.

The name seemed unfamiliar to her. She had been wafted back in time again; she was Ceci Gramont, wounded unto death by the accusation which yet rang in her ears, "Harlot! Harlot!" Then she realized that he was gone and she alone. There was grace in that. Gervais, for all of his subsequent kindness and forebearance, had played the maidservant to a shrinking, embarrassed Ceci—gently removing her garments until she had stood naked under eyes that roved up and down her body before he had carried her to the bed.

Rose was in the room, excited and tremulous, but beyond murmuring her felicitations, she said nothing as, smilingly, she prepared Celia for bed, arraying her in a long, lacy nightgown and a thin silk peignoir. Then she was gone, and Celia surprised at her absence—for she had not really noticed her departure.

She remained at her dressing table—her reticule within easy reach. She glimpsed herself in her mirror—her eyes were huge and blazing, and her hair released from its pins flowed down her back, making her look younger—but not too young, she hoped, not so that he might be too early reminded of Ceci Gramont. Yet, he would not be thinking of that child tonight—her memory would be dimmed by the thought of his present conquest and by the fact of his prior successes—so many unhappy women, Alys had told her once.

She had removed the fine gold chain from her neck before Rose had seen it and the object, which was a ring, lay in her left hand. Clutching it, she rehearsed what she would say and the feel of that concealed ring gave her courage. She hoped he would—all speculations ceased. The door was opening.

He was wearing a long brocade dressing gown and he was looking toward the bed. "I am here," Celia told him and was surprised that her voice was not quite steady. She thought it must be her interior excitement because she was no longer frightened—she was only glad that all pretense would soon be at an end.

He turned. "My love, my dear love." He came toward her, hands outstretched.

She made no move to grasp them. She said, "I have something to give you."

"Your beautiful self."

"More than that, Armin."

"I want only you." He moved closer to her.

"But you must have this." She stretched out her hand. "You have given me the betrothal ring and you may have this in return—it was never mine to keep, you told me that . . . and I know you will be glad to have it back in your possession." She had delivered the speech she had rehearsed and now she thrust the ring into his hand and, feeling the warmth of his fingers, she drew back with a little gasp; she had had an odd tingling sensation—one she had never experienced before.

He was staring at her in a puzzled way. "What is this . . . ? I do not understand."

She moved the candelabra on the dressing table toward him. "Look at it," she invited. "I am sure you must recognize it. Though you wrote that it did not have much monetary value, you also described it as an heirloom of great significance to your family, it being a present from Sir Thomas More."

He thrust his open palm into the light, looking at the ring incredulously. Then he shifted his gaze to her face. "Where . . . did you find . . . this?"

"You do recognize it, I see," she said dryly.

"Where did you get it?"

"It was given me," she returned steadily.

"By whom?" He rapped the question at her.

She was tense now, but lifting her chin, she met his perplexed gaze. "You, my Lord. You wanted it returned. Well, you have it, and I have this." She held up her hand, and for the second time that night she noted rainbow gleams upon the walls. "At last you have replaced it with your— betrothal ring."

He stepped back. "You . . . you are telling me that you, Celia Grayce, are . . ."

"Ceci Gramont?" She flung the name at him. "Yes, that is what I am telling you. I am sorry that I wed you under an assumed name—but it was not quite assumed. My full name is Cecilia Grace, and though I have used Gramont, I have no more right to it than I have to the Grayce since my father did not see fit to wed my mother. The Chadbourne is, however, quite legitimate, conferred upon me by a man, who was, I imagine you might say, less proud than the scion of the Sherlay house—though if Gervais were alive, I think he would provide an argument, there."

"It . . . it is not possible . . . you are nothing like . . ."

"You are ill served by your memory, but, indeed why should you recall so trifling an incident? However, it is possible. Ceci Gramont is ten years older."

"You . . . she was so little . . ."

"In common with my late brother George, I received my growth after sixteen—yes, I was sixteen, not seventeen, when I met you in the park. I am taller. My face has lengthened and an illness left my hair as you see it. Yet I

am she whom you dubbed harlot." She touched her cheek.
"I am sure that even you must remember that confrontation,
my Lord." She regarded him coldly, but at the sight of his
white, still face and furious eyes, her hand inched toward
her reticule.

"Why?" he mouthed at last.

"Surely, there's little need to explain—why?" She made
herself smile brightly, and as her fingers fastened on the
silk of her reticule, she hoped that her expression was suf-
ficiently triumphant. Yet, in spite of her resolution, she was
frightened. Still, she dared to broaden her smile, and rising,
picked up the reticule. "I fear you are angered, my Lord,
but you are not quite the loser, are you? At least you have
Sir Thomas' ring." She could not conceal a start as he shook
his fist—but he was not shaking his fist, she realized as the
ring struck the stone of the fireplace, fell with a clatter to
the floor, and bounced across it. She took an involuntary
step backward, feeling the edge of the dressing table behind
her, impeding all further movement. She fumbled with the
strings of the reticule, only to have him step foward and
wrest it from her, throwing it to the floor. It fell with a hard
thud. He laughed. "Did you think to shoot me or stab me?"

"I thought to protect myself," she cried defiantly and
dared to try to retrieve it, but springing forward, he seized
her in his arms and bore her toward the bed.

Putting both hands against his chest, she tried to thrust
him back but to no avail—she could not break a hold which
had nothing of the gentleness with which he had carried her
into the house. "Let me go, let me go, you cannot want me
now!" she cried between trembling lips.

"On the contrary, Madame," he said between his teeth,
"I do want you—when a man buys the services of a harlot,
he deserves some return for his money."

"You insult me," she exclaimed. "You must know that
I only did this because . . . because . . ."

"Do not trouble to give me reasons, doxy." His laugh
was loud and out of control. "And pray tell me how one

might insult a Cyprian—only by not meeting her price, and I have met yours, have I not, my lovely drab? I have paid well for this night of ecstacy." Throwing her to the bed, he knelt beside her, his hands rending the thin silk of her peignoir and nightgown.

Seeing his face in the glow of the firelight, she thought it looked murderous. Terror thrilled through her and again she strove to escape him, only to be caught and pressed against the bed, held easily with one strong hand while, with the other, he divested himself of his own garments. Then, falling upon her, he pinioned her beneath him.

He was breathing heavily, and though she beat against his chest with both fists and dared to drive her nails into his bare shoulders, she was unable to contend against his strength. His lips were on her mouth, and inexorably, her thighs were being kneed apart—yet feeling his hard muscular body bearing down upon her, incredibly, her fear gave way to some deep, primitive response that she could not control and, within a few moments, did not want to control. Her body began to move in an effortless rhythm that matched his own. It was something she had never been able to achieve with Gervais—with her first husband, she had lain still, accepting his advances. Hating and fearing Armin, she yet responded to his every practiced touch, welcoming it, craving it, and with the throbbing, the hardening, and the thrusting, all conscious thought ceased and, for the first time in her life, she was lifted upward, outside of herself, before finally falling into a delicious exhaustion at his side, but she was ready and welcoming at a second possession and a third. Then, amazingly, toward morning, he grew gentler, kissing her with a strange tenderness, little kisses that fell on mouth and throat and breasts—caresses that she returned until, exhausted, she fell asleep in his arms.

Late that following morning, Celia awakened to find herself alone. She was disappointed. She had wanted him to be at her side. Her body was aching but that did not matter. She edged toward the spot where he had lain and imagined his arms around her and without thinking, she murmured, "I love him."

She was startled by the admission—she tried to refute it. She had thought she did not love him, but she did and knew, now, the reason she had wanted to exact her revenge. Beneath all her hatred, there had been love—she had loved him all her life, still loved him in spite of all that had happened. To think of the previous night was to feel as if she had been born again—as if her body were new and she new, too, another person with all of her old hatreds gone and only the memory of his tenderness left. Then, she remembered what she had told him and was frightened—he still did not know the truth, but did that matter? He had proved that he loved her, had he not? She would tell him the whole of the story that morning—let him understand why she had been so angry and so hurt. Determinedly, she moved toward the edge of the bed. She was about to get up when she was halted by a knock on the door. Probably it was Rose . . . she slipped beneath the covers again. "Come," she called.

It was not Rose who entered. It was Lord Sherlay. He had evidently been riding, for he was wearing buckskin breeches and high leather riding boots. His jacket was draped over his shoulders and his hair was tousled by the wind. A greeting rose to her lips and was quelled by his expression—there was nothing of tenderness in it. His eyes were marble hard and his mouth grim. He seemed to be looking at her, but actually she found his glance to be fixed on a point above her head. In accents so cold they chilled her to the bone, he said, "I have come to offer my apologies. I was much angered last night. I will not refine upon what took place—other than to assure you that it will not happen again."

"I . . . I expect," she began, and was amazed at the effort it cost her to say, "that you want a divorce."

"No, Madame," he said harshly. "It may no doubt surprise you, but that did not enter my mind. There never has been a divorce in my family and I'll not crown this latest folly by one I believe to be even worse. We shall enjoy what is known as a 'fashionable marriage.' You will have your apartments in this house. You will forgive me if I do not take you to Briarton Abbey—I could not shame the memory of my mother in that way. Consequently, we shall remain in town and I shall occupy a suite down the hall. We will see each other only when it is absolutely necessary—such as when we are required to appear at Carlton House or at other similar functions. Aside from that, we will live separately and pursue our separate ways. You will not interfere with my life and I'll not interfere with yours. I ask only that you endeavor to be discreet. You have been pleased to exact your revenge. It is useless for me to tell you what I think of that or you. Suffice to say that since you bear my name, I shall expect that you will observe the rules of proper social conduct—as much as a woman of your stamp is capable of doing. Is that agreeable?"

She had listened in growing anger. Again, he had not troubled to ask her why she had resorted to such desperate measures—nor did he want to hear her side of the matter. As on that other occasion, a decade earlier, he had merely assumed that she was a hardened courtesan. In tones as cold as those he had employed, she said, "The rules of conduct you have suggested were those I expected to follow were I to remain here. However, I had thought a divorce must be the inevitable result of what I chose to do. Since you have decided that for your pride, you prefer not to pursue such a course, I shall remain your wife until such time as you see fit to change your mind. It might be, my Lord, that you will eventually find another female with whom you can be more comfortable. If this occurs, I shall gladly relinquish all claim to your name."

"That is very magnaminous of you, Madame. I will keep your offer in mind, and now . . . if you will excuse me?"

"Certainly," she said.

With a small bow, he was gone and Celia, staring after

him dry-eyed, shivered. Someone had opened a window and the November winds were very cold—she dragged the covers around her, and as she did, she caught sight of the diamond on her finger—it glittered like an icicle or a teardrop. She hated it. She pulled it off . . . then, she slipped it on again. She had promised to abide by the outward forms of their marriage and this was one of them. It was also a reminder that Ceci Gramont had won, and in winning had forfeited everything that might have made Celia Chadbourne happy.

— **Part Three** —

9

SNOW MIXED WITH rain was making the streets very slippery. Though conditions were better than they had been during the last stormy days of the old year, Sir Hugo Clavering, standing at the window of a small house on Eyre Street, looked anxiously at swirling flakes illuminated by the glow from a gas lamp outside. He cast a glance over his shoulder at the table where Lady Sherlay was playing hazard. He hoped she was ready to leave, but she was as intent on the game as she had been when he had stopped beside her twenty minutes earlier.

It was difficult driving in this weather. Lord Alvanley's matched grays had fallen on the ice-coated pavements of Regent Street, overturning his chaise and injuring both the coachman and the boots; fortunately, his Lordship had been at Whites. Though Sir Hugo counted his own coachman a better hand with the ribbons, still ice was always a threat and the Sherlay mansion a good distance away. He hoped Lady Sherlay was not losing—for that circumstance only served to keep her at the tables longer. In the past month, her vaunted luck had been only intermittent and she had lost as much as she had won. However, far from being cast down by this circumstance, she had gambled incessantly, playing at the houses of friends, acquaintances—anywhere, indeed, where the game was constant and deep.

Thinking about it, he frowned. It was true that she had enjoyed gaming before her marriage, but in the two months since her wedding she seemed to have developed a veritable passion for it. Furthermore, she had hinted that though her husband did not approve of her obsession, she was not going to mind his strictures. "I have done as I choose too long to stop at his command," she had informed Sir Hugo with a toss of her head. She had spoken lightly and smiled. It seemed to him that she did a great deal more laughing and smiling than she had when he had first known her. In fact, since her marriage, her temperament seemed to have changed completely—in place of her quiet serenity was a hectic gaiety which disturbed him. However, her Lord had not changed at all. Much to the surprise of the *ton*, he had begun a liaison with a Miss Peggy Charke, a pert young actress new this season to Drury Lane. Indeed, not two weeks after his marriage, he was to be seen sitting in a box over the stage gazing boldly at his new love, who did not scruple to step out of character long enough to blow kisses back at him—and if that were not shocking enough, he had committed the social solecism of holding a long conversation with her while she sat in her carriage at Hyde Park Corner during the fashionable hour of five. Fortunately, his wife had not been present. It was noted that they were seldom together. In fact, he could think of only two occasions when Lord Sherlay had appeared by the side of his wife—one being a dinner at Carlton House and the other a ball at the same establishment. It was noted that on the latter occasion he had danced only once with Lady Sherlay. However, she had not lacked for partners, for she had, as usual, looked ravishingly beautiful.

She was looking lovely tonight—she had taken to wearing a great deal of blue and the gown she had chosen was precisely the color of her eyes. The diamond and sapphire necklace she had worn at her wedding sparkled on her throat. Thinking of that wedding, he shook his head, wondering why Lord Sherlay, whose prejudice against marriage had seemingly matched that of his friend Sir Charles Vandrington, had wed her. It was a question all the *ton* had asked in the last two months—but the only two who might have given them a proper answer were singularly noncommital. However, one thing was certain—it was not an alliance that had been made in Heaven.

Sir Hugo looked down at his hand, surprised that his palm was stinging, and realized that he had slammed his fist against it in a burst of untypical anger. He had never liked Sherlay and now he was perilously close to loathing him. It was a new emotion for him—generally, his disposition tended to be placid—but though one could never guess it from her demeanor, he was sure that Lady Sherlay was unhappy. For one thing, her constant laughter was never reflected in her eyes. For another, there were moments when she actually seemed to be forcing herself to speak, and more than once he had glimpsed a brooding look in her eyes, until becoming aware of his scrutiny, she had either become interested in some object—a china ornament or a picture or even someone across the room—or she smiled brightly and made some light comment, either attitude assumed in order to deflect his attention from herself. He wished fervently that he knew her well enough to be in her confidence—but he did not. He darted another glance at the table and saw to his relief that she had risen and was scanning the room, evidently searching for him. He hurried to her side.

"Are you ready to leave, Lady Sherlay?"

"Yes." She smiled.

"I hope your luck was in."

"In and out—I broke even or very nearly. The Luck is that way—it comes and goes. Fortunately, there is always

another night." She rested her hand on his arm. "Take me
home, dear Sir Hugo, and thank you for waiting so patiently."

"You thank me for little, but I do wish . . ."

"If wishes were horses, beggars would ride. If turnips
were watches, I doubt if they would keep good time. Come,
I confess myself weary at last."

"At once, my Lady," he said obediently.

Murmuring a series of polite farewells, she made her
way across the chamber and, following her, Sir Hugo was
even more concerned than before. He had read desperation
in her eyes and he feared she had lost a great deal more
than she admitted. He wondered what the disapproving Lord
Sherlay would have to say to that. Then, with another
twinge of that unfamiliar fury, he wished that he might be
there when she confronted her husband. If Lord Sherlay
were to say one harsh word to her, he, Hugo Clavering,
would be delighted to thrust those words back into his gullet
with his bare fists!

In spite of her warm cloak and the shawl she had tied over
her turban, Celia was shivering as she bade farewell to Sir
Hugo in the hallway of Sherlay House. It being late, the
fire had died down to a mass of gray embers, but once
Bellows had closed the door behind Sir Hugo, she still
hurried to the hearth to hold out her fingers.

"Should Milady wish another log to be set upon the fire?"
the butler inquired respectfully.

"No, unless . . . has his Lordship returned?"

"Yes, Milady, sometime since."

"Then—never mind any extra wood." She smiled. "And
please go to bed, I am sorry I am so late. You must be tired
and poor Rose, too."

"It is of no matter, your Ladyship." The butler bowed.
"Good night, your Ladyship."

"Good night, Bellows." She went up the stairs slowly.

She was very tired but she welcomed that feeling for it meant she might sleep more soundly than was her wont of late. Reaching the second landing, she paused to catch her breath. She was not usually so winded. Inadvertently, she glanced down the long corridor. His suite lay at the end of it, he had moved there the night following their arrival. She was surprised that he was home—more than once, she had lain wakeful listening for the sound of his footsteps on the stair and had been rewarded by a silence broken only by the sound of the large clock in the hall as relentlessly it struck the hours away. There had been times when she had heard his step and the closing of his door. In the beginning, she had longed to go to him and confess the whole of her folly but that, in itself, would have been folly—for the face he turned toward her was that of a stranger—just as whatever words he addressed to her were few and coldly polite. To think of the nights she had gone with him to Carlton House was to remember the silent journey in the chaise and the silent return.

In spite of her promise to remain under his roof, it was a strain that was telling on her physically as well as mentally. She was not feeling her best—there had been times when she had been quite vaporish. One possibility for her disorder had presented itself to her—but she was quick to dismiss it. In nine years of marriage to Gervais she had not conceived, and since the late Lady Drusilla Chadbourne had had three miscarriages beside the one son who had grown to manhood, she knew that the fault was hers. Undoubtedly, her present symptoms rose out of her unhappiness. She wished she could hate him as much as she had at Torleigh Manor and knew that she had not hated him even then, and to meet him even as infrequently as she did, and see his face set in those harsh lines, was an agony she had never anticipated.

She turned toward her room and as she did, the door to the library, which lay between their two suites, opened and he stepped into the hall. He was carrying a book, and as his eyes fell on her they widened. "You are only now arriving home?"

"Only now," she acknowledged coldly.

"It is late."

"Yes."

"You led me to believe that you had gone to the Houghtons' on Eyre Street."

"That was my destination."

He took a step forward. "Did you arrive?"

"Where else might I go?"

His expression was grim. "I do not pretend to know your mind, Madame."

She lifted her chin. "If you have doubts about me, my Lord, I suggest you hire one of the Bow Street Runners and have me followed."

"That does not answer my question as to where you were this evening."

"As I informed you earlier, I was at Lord and Lady Houghton's on Eyre Street. Sir Hugo has just brought me home."

There was no change in his expression. "I presume you gambled."

"Yes."

"Did you win?"

"No, but since my money is my own to use as I wish, you need not be concerned over my losses."

A slight smile lifted the corners of his mouth. "But what has happened to the famous Chadbourne Luck, Madame? Have you fallen in love and has the Devil punished you?"

"You may believe what you choose, my Lord."

Just for a moment the look in his eyes was murderous, and then he shrugged. "You must remember that you promised to be discreet."

"I have been discreet, my Lord," she said, and turning on her heel, she walked into her chamber. She half feared he might follow, but he did not. A wave of dizziness came over her and she had barely time to step to her bed. Sitting down hastily, she clutched the post while the room seemed to circle about her. Dimly, she heard Rose's sleepy voice sharpen with anxiety. "Milady, Milady, what is amiss?"

The queasiness dissipated and she managed a smile. "Nothing, Rose, my dear. Pray undress me. I am sure you must be much in need of sleep."

"Might I not fetch you a cordial or some wine, Milady?"

"Nothing, child. See, I am quite myself again."

Though the girl ceased to protest, she still looked anxious and she was very gentle in her ministrations. Finally, she was gone and Celia in bed. Lying there in the dark, she pondered on what had just passed between herself and her husband. Had he been waiting for her to come home? The library faced the street—had he stood at the window watching for Sir Hugo's chaise—or had he merely heard her footsteps as she came up the stairs? The latter explanation was undoubtedly the right one. Yet, it had been surprising to find him in the library so late at night—or rather, so early in the morning, it being past three. Had he been concerned about her? That was unlikely—he had been at great pains to show her that he now cared nothing for her. Had he actually believed that she had been returning from some assignation? For a moment, she was furious to think that he could have entertained such a suspicion, but her fury soon passed. Had she not encouraged such beliefs herself? Yet, could he not see . . . No, he could see nothing, for she had encased the real Celia in a veil of lies. Why could she not have realized that she loved him—if she had been aware of that, she would have thrown that stupid ring into the Thames and Ceci Gramont would have gone with it—drowned in the past. But Ceci had not wanted that— still did not want it. He should know the real truth—all the truth, but he would never hear it from her and there was no one else could tell him.

For a fleeting instant, she was sorry that she had broken with her sister. If they had been on friendly terms, she might have written to Bella, who in turn could have written to Lord Sherlay, but it was not Bella who must needs rescue her from the pit she had dug for herself—the grave, rather— and besides, the grim hard man in the hall was conditioned against any belief in her.

Thinking of the contemptuous way in which he had addressed her, she murmured, "I hate him," and wished it were true. Turning over, she buried her face in her pillow and closed her eyes; she needed to sleep, but the clock had struck seven before she finally fell into a slumber that lasted no more than two hours, which was unfortunate, for it was one of those evenings when she was due to make an appearance with her husband at a Carlton House ball, the first of the New Year.

Never had the ballroom at Carlton House seemed so bright; the huge mirrors reflected dancers whirling to a sprightly new waltz. To Celia, held lightly in the arms of Sir Charles Vandrington, those figures seemed to merge into one great mass of color and glitter. Though she smiled dutifully, she was conscious of dizziness, and though the festivities were scarcely underway, she wished they were at an end—but they would not be—not for many hours, and though her legs ached and her feet burned, her dances were all bespoken by gentlemen who had crowded around her like bees at a honeycomb. In spite of her nearly sleepless night, she was aware that she was looking her best.

Rose had arranged her hair to accommodate a diamond tiara ornamented with rubies, and her gown, a scarlet velvet in the new, fuller body, was stitched with gold at the hem and bosom. Rubies glowed on her throat, wrist, and fingers. There had been murmurs of approbation when she had appeared on Lord Sherlay's arm—but he for whom she had donned the gown had given it the briefest of glances as he had held out her cloak and, as usual, he had made no comment. But it was a sheer waste of time to dwell on reactions to which she had become accustomed. She sighed and, glancing upward, met the enigmatic gaze of her partner. As usual, she felt uncomfortable with him. Though he had been full of easy compliments, he had uttered them in a tone of voice that had seemed to suggest that he was only paying lip service to a convention that required such transports from gentlemen. She wondered what he really thought of her and decided quickly that she did not want to know. Then, as he whirled her about in a complicated turn, the dizziness was upon her again. Coming to a stop, she clutched his arm. "If you please . . ." she breathed.

Before she could say another word, he had quickly led her across the floor and into the corridor, where he hastily opened a window. "Breathe deeply," he commanded.

The air was icy enough to sear her nostrils but she could tell him gratefully, "That does make me feel much more the thing. I thank you."

"*Pas de quoi*," he drawled. "It seems that rescuing you has become a habit of mine."

"I am much in your debt." She smiled. "I expect we'd best go back . . ."

"Tarry a moment longer," he urged. "It is very warm in the ballroom. His Royal Highness has a penchant for the overdone and the overheated." He glanced at the heavy gold leaf on the high ceilings. "Besides, there is something I would ask you."

For some indefinable reason, she was frightened, but she said easily enough, "What might that be, Sir Charles?"

"One has heard that you are a most determined gamester. Is that true?"

"Yes, it is the truth."

There was a gleam in his gray eyes. "One has also heard that you are the possessor of the Chadbourne Luck."

"I have been." She shrugged.

"And now . . . are not?"

"I have been only intermittently lucky of late."

"Ah, that is a pity. I had hoped . . ." He shook his head. "But never mind."

"What had you hoped, Sir Charles?"

"That you might play with me, but if you are afraid . . ."

"Afraid?" she echoed. "Why should I be afraid?"

"If you have lost the Luck . . ."

"It's not entirely lost . . . I have won as well as lost."

"Then—you do not feel yourself entirely bereft of it?"

"No, I do not."

"Should you care to play with me, then?"

She was conscious of a great relief and realized that this was not the request, she had anticipated. She did not stop to speculate as to what she might have expected him to ask. She merely said, "I should be delighted."

"I warn you that I play for high stakes."

"As do I," she returned calmly.

"We must set a time and a place. I hope it may be soon."

"Tomorrow evening, I shall be visiting Lady Torleigh . . . I am told there will be tables of piquet."

"I know there will be tables of piquet—I am bound there myself tomorrow night. Might I escort you?"

"No, I am going with Sir Hugo Clavering."

"So be it—perhaps another time." He offered his arm. "Are you ready to return?"

"Yes, quite ready." She could have added 'more than ready,' for, as usual, she was feeling edgy and uneasy in his presence. However, it might be exciting to play cards with him. That, in itself, was the greatest inducement, for since her marriage, excitement was a word that had lost all meaning and with it had gone anticipation and, of course, happiness. Hope, however, remained—the one, forlorn hope that time would eventually pass more quickly, hurrying her toward her grave.

The Torleighs had hired a snug house on King Street and if it was not as large as Lady Alys would have liked, it was warm and comfortable and one of its two drawing rooms sufficed as a ballroom, provided there were not too many dancers. The other drawing room was given over to those who wished to play cards. However, it being past midnight, most of the party were finishing what everyone agreed was a sumptuous supper—for the Torleighs had brought Jacques up to town and that night he had surpassed even himself.

The hostess, moving toward the door, was stopped and complimented by numerous of her guests. She acknowledged these encomiums gratefully but continued on her way, emerging into the hall and looking about her frowningly. Her brow cleared as she sighted the object of her search and moved toward a bench at the far end of the corridor. "Celia, my dear, are you not well, then?"

Celia looked up quickly. "I am quite well, Alys . . . it was only a little close in there."

"I was watching you. Have you decided to disapprove of my poor Jacques?"

"Of course not. Why do you ask?"

"You hardly touched the soup or the chicken or any of the side dishes. I am glad he was not there to watch, else he must have thrown down his hat and stamped on it. He is a very temperamental man and highly sensitive to criticism."

"I cannot imagine anyone criticizing him," Celia assured her. "I am not very hungry. I am sure that Jacques cannot complain of the condition in which most of the plates have been returned."

"One dissenting opinion is equal to all the assenting ones in the eyes of any artist. Are you not well?"

"Very well."

"Good . . . should you like to play a game of piquet with me?"

"Actually, I had promised to play with Sir Charles Vandrington. I must confess I am surprised that he is not here."

"Vandrington! I should not advise you to play cards with him. He is a cold, calculating, and ruthless gamester—with a passion for winning and infernal luck. Last year, young Northbrugh lost the whole of his fortune to him in a single evening at Boodles. He blew his brains out the next day."

"I promise you, I'll not follow his example." Celia smiled.

"One hears that the Luck . . . ." Lady Alys began.

"Is not holding," Celia finished. "That is my fault. I have been preoccupied from time to time, and if you'll promise not to betray me, I shall tell you that the famous Luck is based upon a certain system which requires a knowledge of what has been played. Its secret is simply concentration."

Lady Alys' eyes were round with amazement. "That is the truth?"

"That is the truth, and when I concentrate, I generally win. I promise you that I shall not fail to concentrate when paired with Sir Charles."

Lady Alys eyed her dubiously. "Why are you so eager to play with him? He frightens me."

"You, also?"

"Does he frighten you, then?"

"I—find him intimidating, yes, though I've no reason for it. Perhaps it's merely his choice of garments."

"They are depressing, but there's more to it than that."

"Still . . . I am sure the game will prove exciting."

"I do not understand you, Celia . . . gaming never used to mean so much to you."

"They have said that it's a fever in the blood—perhaps I have caught it."

"My dear," Lady Alys began commiseratingly, "I cannot help but feel that there is something preying . . ."

"Lady Torleigh, my abject apologies to you and to you also, Lady Sherlay."

The two young women turned to find Vandrington coming toward them. "Sir Charles!" Lady Alys rose quickly, followed by Celia, "I had begun to think . . . ."

"I am sure that I can guess what you had begun to think," he interrupted, "but I must tell you that my lateness was not of my doing. On the way here, I had an unfortunate encounter in the streets."

"Unfortunate? An accident to your coach?" Lady Alys demanded.

"No, I was walking and met a pair of footpads."

"You walked!" Lady Alys exclaimed, looking at him incredulously.

"Always on these clear brisk nights."

"I pray you were not injured," Celia said.

"You are more than kind, Lady Sherlay. No, I was not . . . but the Watch was most put out and it was he delayed me."

"The Watch?" Lady Alys questioned.

"Ah, you seem surprised, as was I—for what might one do with a body? He could hardly expect me to cart it to the . . . wherever one . . . carts bodies. However, I bested him in the argument. I told him that if it was not his duty to protect pedestrians from such exigencies, he might at least clear the debris away."

"You killed the thieves!" Celia exclaimed.

"Alas, only one of them . . . the other took to his heels before I could reload my pistol. But enough of that. I hope I am forgiven for the delay?"

"Of course." Lady Alys looked at him with awe. "What a horrid thing to happen."

"Hardly unusual, though. My only regret has been that it kept me far too long away from a pleasure I have been anticipating. I hope, Lady Sherlay, that you'll not tell me I am too tardy for our promised game?"

"Certainly not," she replied, with a coolness that matched his own. "I, too, have been anticipating it, Sir Charles."

Despite Lady Alys' warnings and despite her own fluctuating fortunes, Celia was not without confidence as she sat down to play. She had told no more than the truth when she had said that the Luck was purely a matter of concentration. It was obvious to her that her own recent difficulties had arisen out of an inability to fix her mind on the game.

However, the thought of playing with Vandrington put her on her mettle and, in the beginning of their match, it seemed as if the Chadbourne Luck remained in her possession. Though he was an excellent player, she won sixty points for repique in the first rubber and achieved a similar gain during the third. Then, suddenly, her luck turned.

Celia did not know how it had happened, but once Vandrington gained an ascendancy he did not lose his advantage. By the time the match was drawing to a close, she was trembling—but not so much at the thought of her losses, which were considerable, but because of the man who sat across from her. There was something so repellent about him that she could not keep her mind on the game. She was not sure why he had had such an effect on her. It might have been his singularly penetrating gaze, which seemed to bore through flesh and bone to the very convolutions of her mind, or it may have been the way he moved his hands, which seemed too small for the rest of his body—small, deft, darting, they reminded her of two snakes, a comparison which, on the face of it, was ridiculous. Yet, with his narrow head, slender body, and gray garments, there was something serpentine about the entire man and, judging from this night's adventure, also lethal. Though she had lost over five thousand pounds, it was a relief for her to lay down her cards and say with a shrug, "I have been worsted by a master."

"On the contrary," he replied, "I do not claim such superiority over a player as skilled as yourself, Lady Sherlay. I thought you must offer a challenge and you did."

"Come"—she smiled—"I think I offered you very little in the way of that."

"Not true, and certainly it was a great pleasure to sit across from you. You must give me the opportunity of doing so again."

She shook her head. "I think not, Sir Charles."

"No? I cannot believe that you are craven, Lady Sherlay."

"Nor am I, but that which I lose belongs to my late husband's estate—and I'd not dig too deeply into funds which were left to me for land improvement and the like."

"Ah, that I can understand and I applaud it—but I should like to propose a different stake."

"A different stake?" she repeated with a little throb of fear, though why she should be frightened she did not understand.

"To be near you—is to wish to be nearer yet, Lady Sherlay. I would give all I have won tonight to enjoy your . . . favors. That is the stake I propose."

"My . . . favors," she whispered, staring at him incredulously. "How dare you suggest . . . I thought you were my husband's friend."

"Of a truth, I am, but I cannot think he would complain were I to enjoy his leavings . . . he has not a selfish nature, poor Sherlay."

"His . . ." She would have risen, but with a movement as swift as any striking snake, he clamped a hand upon her wrist.

"Stay, my love—can you believe I do not know what you have done? You've been very clever and you possessed the Luck, but I, too, am lucky, as you learned tonight. It but remains to see which luck will win tomorrow night—when we play at Sherlay House—for your husband will be from home, having forsaken his solitary couch for the bower of the fair Miss Charke, who appears at Drury Lane. As you see, I enjoy much of his confidence."

"He . . . he t-told you that . . ."

"That you wove a shiny little silken web around him? No, my dear, for his pride, he did not. But you see, I guessed. I was well acquainted with the late Sir Harry Gramont and, in consequence, I knew about his nest of by-blows—including the lovely Arabella, whose favors Lord Madreston used to enjoy. I might add, my dear, that while you have something of the look of your sister, you are even more to my taste. You have grown so much more beautiful—I noticed that the night I rescued you from the Prince, which you might have mistaken for disinterested chivalry, which I assure you, my dear, it was not. It was enough even for me to risk the Prince's displeasure when I consider how much it pleasured me."

She tried to wrench her wrist away, but his grasp only tightened, hurting her. "Let me go," she whispered furiously.

"Softly, softly, my dear. Anger will serve you ill. Best do as I ask. After all, you have possessed the Chadbourne Luck and might be lucky tomorrow night. If so, you'll have your five thousand pounds again and the promise of my silence on a matter which, if printed in the *Morning Post*, would afford no end of amusement to the gossips among the *haut ton*, though I cannot believe it would have so salubrious an effect upon the Sherlay pride."

"And you call yourself his friend?" she whispered.

"I'd rather call myself your lover—but I may yet be the loser. The choice is yours, my beautiful. And though I am not a poet, I find a rhyme running through my head—something about a game or shame? Which will it be, my sweet angel?"

"And if I win?" she asked.

"You win all."

"How can I believe that?"

"You have my word."

"I do not trust your word, Sir Charles."

His gray eyes hardened, "If you lose, I'll make you regret those words."

"I am counting on not losing."

"Then—I shall give you a writ which you may show. Is that agreeable?"

"Yes."

"So be it."

"Release my wrist."

"I shall, but smile at me, my dear. We are not unobserved."

She gave a quick glance around the room. Though many of the tables were deserted, some few players remained, among them Lady Alys, who, fortunately, was not looking in her direction. Rising, she forced a smile. "I thank you for the game, Sir Charles. But now I—I must find poor Sir Hugo . . . I am a little weary."

"That is understandable, Lady Sherlay." He rose and bowed. "You must let me escort you from the room."

"There's no need."

"On the contrary," he said in a low voice, "there is every need—else they might think you a bad loser."

Steeling herself, she put her hand lightly on his arm and suffered him to lead her forth into the corridor. She moved away from him hastily then. "I am sure Sir Hugo is in the ballroom. I . . . I will seek him there. Good night, Sir Charles."

"Good night, my dear, I shall wait upon you tomorrow evening. Will you name a time?"

"Nine?"

"Nine it will be—and may the better of us win." Bowing, he went down the stairs.

Starting toward the ballroom, Celia found her knees weak and she sank down upon a chair. She had an impulse to run from the house, run until she reached Chadbourne Hall, but it could prove no haven now—and Lord Sherlay would be the sufferer if she vanished. She had no doubt but that Sir Charles would carry out his threat. She must stay and take her chances—she had no choice.

The immense interior of the Drury Lane was brightly lighted and its pit, boxes, and gallery filled to overflowing with a noisy and convivial crowd come to watch *A Winter's Tale*, which was a favorite—especially when the delectable Miss Peggy Charke appeared in the role of Perdita.

> "Sir, my gracious Lord,
> To chide at your extremes it not becomes me;

O, pardon that I name them! your high self,
The gracious mark of the land, you have obscured
With a swain's wearing and me, poor lowly maid,
Most goddess like prank'd up, but that our feasts
In every mess have folly and the feeders
Digest it with a custom. I should blush
To see you so attired, I think,
To show myself a glass."

That Miss Peggy Charke, looking particularly fetching
in the sprigged muslin gown which she had chosen as a
costume likely to be worn by Perdita, spoke those lines to
the handsome man in the box directly over the stage rather
than to her Florizel, was enough to earn her a hissed, "Look
at *me*, damn you" from the enraged actor.

She pouted but obediently stared at him as he declaimed,
"'I bless the time when my good falcon made her flight
above thy father's ground.'"

"'Now Jove afford your cause!'" began Miss Charke,
twirling her beribboned shepherd's crook. "'To me the difference forges dread; your greatness . . .'" And here she
sent another languishing look at that box only to pause
midspeech and stare indignantly at a lovely young woman,
who had that moment appeared in Milord's box and was
clutching his arm, staring at him in obvious distress. It put
her right off her speech and out of her character as well,
as she watched open-mouthed and unmindful of her Florizel's whispered injunctions.

The ensuing pause set those members of the gallery who
had been hanging on her words as well as admiring her
beauty to muttering angrily while their neighbors in the pit
let loose a hail of rotten vegetables. These served as an
inducement to bring Miss Charke to her senses. Avoiding
a large tomato which landed with a splat upon a painted
Arcadian glade, she declaimed the remainder of her speech
with a fervor which she hoped would quiet the patrons and,
at the same time, keep the wrath of the manager from

descending upon her golden head. It did not improve her
state of mind when, during Florizel's next speech, she dared
to dart a glance at the box only to find it empty. She did
not hesitate to attribute Milord's defection to the young
woman, who, judging from her appearance, was a member
of the *ton*—but her behavior had been confusing. Surely
ladies of quality were not in the habit of accosting gentlemen
in their boxes, midperformance. It was certainly most surprising.

Lord Sherlay, looking down into Lady Alys' troubled
eyes, unconsciously shared Miss Charke's surprise. "My
dear Lady Alys," he began, only to be interrupted by Lord
Rolf, who at that moment appeared in the corridor, looking
much out of countenance.

"By God, Alys," he began explosively, "I . . ."

"I will say it," she cried. "I know what I heard and what
I saw . . . and I am sure she was frightened."

"But, my dear, you cannot . . ."

"Who was frightened?" Lord Sherlay interposed.

"I tell you," Lord Rolf protested, "it's not fitting   "

"Rolf, please," Lady Alys begged. She looked up at
Lord Sherlay beseechingly. "Luck or no luck, she's no
match for Vandrington. I was in the cardroom last night
and saw him win . . . he'll do the same tonight and I know
she does not want to play with him. I saw her face . . . she
looked so distressed and I know she went down heavily—
for he always plays for high stakes. Then—when he led her
out of the cardroom, I followed and heard him say he'd
come to her at nine . . . at least she said it must be nine
. . . but there was such a horrid look on his face and she
. . . Oh, Lord Sherlay, I know he's a friend of yours, but
please, that game must be stopped."

Lord Sherlay raised his eyebrows, "Vandrington is gaming with my wife?"

"Yes," she blurted. "And I have such a bad feeling about
it. Please, cannot you interfere?"

"I do not see how that is possible, Lady Alys. You see,

I've promised not to interfere. I do not see how I can go back on my word."

She glared at him. "You'll do nothing?"

He shrugged. "I think, perhaps, your alarm is misplaced, dear Lady Alys, though, of course, I appreciate your concern."

"But . . ."

"My dear." Lord Rolf took her arm and, giving Sherlay an embarrassed glance, he bowed. "I pray you'll excuse us, my Lord . . . females . . ." With an expressive shrug and a roll of his eyes, he hurried his wife down the corridor, while Lord Sherlay stepped back into his box and, much to Miss Charke's relief, took his seat again.

Celia, staring at the spread of cards on the table in the library, felt as if her insides had been drained from her. In the last two hours of play, she had not won even one rubber. Inexorably, the points had piled up against her and then, with infinite satisfaction, Vandrington had said at the end of the third game, "My dear, you are fairly rubiconed."

"Might we . . . we n-not c-continue the play?" she whispered, hating herself for the note of entreaty she had been unable to stifle.

"Come, Lady Sherlay, it was three out of five, and look you, I've won all three. I might also add that I know the secret of the Luck and I fear you're in no mood to achieve the concentration necessary to win." He smiled at her. "I might also tell you that as a lover, you'll not find me untender . . ." Stretching out his hand, he ran it down her arm, and though her sleeve was long and tight, she shuddered.

"I'll not have you touch me," she flared.

"But we agreed upon the stake," he reminded her gently.

"You forced me to it," she accused.

"I did not force you. Indeed, you had a choice. I am sure Sherlay would have recovered from the affront to his vanity.

He has recovered from more grievous wounds. Think of his chagrin when he found you in that Chelsea dovecote and he fancying he loved you. Indeed, I had a hard time convincing him that he should pay a visit to your sister. He was so sure that you were honest."

For a moment, she could not speak. She had always imagined that Lord Sherlay's appearance in her sister's house was at the behest of Mrs. Moulton, though the woman had denied it repeatedly, swearing that she had no notion how he had come to be there "You . . . convinced him. What . . . how . . . did you know?"

"As I have explained, I knew your family, my dear— the *soi-disant* Gramonts—and since you'd furnished him with a location if not a direction, I dismissed your careful tale of an elderly cousin and, as one so often does at Newmarket, I depended upon my intuition—and lo, I was right as I am so often at Newmarket. But come, my love, I am sure we need not dwell upon the past when the future holds such great promise for us both."

Her eyes were full of tears. "I . . . I remember now . . . you were with him that night . . . the gray . . . Oh, why did I not think on it before? Oh, God, what did you tell him?"

"I needed to tell him nothing—he'd but to look around him at the surroundings, the guests and Mrs. Moulton leading you, decked out in your finery like one of Dashwood's nuns—and what he'd left of common sense informed him as to your guile."

"My guile . . ." She wept. "I knew nothing, nothing."

"And of course did not wed him out of fustian, love?"

"I . . ." she began and fell silent under his amused yet penetrating stare.

"It's wise in you—not to offer arguments, my dear, for there's naught you could say that would convince me that it was otherwise. Well, you have had your revenge. I could not save him from that, but surely a little punishment's in order—though when this evening's at an end, I doubt you'll consider it so." Rising swiftly, he came around the table and standing behind her, caught her shoulders.

"No . . . let me go," she sobbed, striving to pull away from him.

"In time, love, in time." His hands slipped down over her arms, and pulling her to her feet, he clasped his hands around her waist, holding her against him. "You are a sweet armful, Ceci Gramont. I knew that directly I saw you in your sister's house. And, in common with the luscious Arabella, made for loving."

His insinuating voice and, the touch of his small white hands were sending shudder after shudder down her body. She tried to twist away from him but to no avail, and then he had lifted her and was bearing her to the sofa near the fire. "No, please . . . please," she begged. "I will give you anything . . . anything . . ."

"My dearest love, you will give me everything," he said softly, as he put her down. "And by the evening's end, I think you'll admit, you've won, not lost." Pinioning her down, he kissed her until her mouth felt bruised, and though she tried to clamp her teeth upon his invading tongue, it was impossible. Pulling back, he struck her across the face. "None of that, my own." He wrenched at the high collar of her gown, and though it was made of heavy silk, he managed to rip it in two. Then his mouth was on her throat and wandering toward her breasts. For a moment, she lay passively—then as his grip loosened, she tried once more to thrust him back—a maneuver which elicited a short laugh from him. "You are full of tricks, my sweet, but before the evening's at an end, depend upon it, you'll have learned some new ones . . ."

She had stopped trying to plead with him. Determinedly, she tried to push him away but he was strong—far stronger than he looked. His hands bit into her flesh like steel talons, and as she well knew, it was no use to struggle for there was no escaping him.

Quite as if he had read her mind, he said, "Best submit with a good grace, my own, else you'll only tire yourself and . . ." His eyes suddenly widened as a cold draught of air smote him. Then the heavy library door crashed against the wall.

"Might I know the meaning of this?" a wrathful voice demanded.

"Armin." Celia slipped out of her attacker's loosened grasp.

Vandrington rose to his feet. "I am sure you need not ask for meanings, Sherlay," he said casually. "You know what you have wed."

"It's not true . . . it's not true," she sobbed, clutching her torn garments against her naked bosom. "He . . . he . . ."

"We played for certain stakes and she lost." Vandrington smiled, then ceased smiling as Lord Sherlay advanced upon him, fists knotted. "I suggest you hold your temper," he said calmly. "I am not a violent man, but—"his hand slipped into his pocket and brought out a small pistol—"but I do believe in self-protection."

"Do you only attack defenseless women, then?" Sherlay grated.

"Defenseless women, no, but whores I find fair game. Now, I'll beg you to come to your senses. Else . . ." He stepped back as Sherlay, with an actual growl, launched himself at him and Celia, seeing the gleam of the metal as he raised the gun, threw herself before her husband. There was a deafening roar, then something hit her violently in the shoulder and she felt herself falling.

"Oh, God, oh, God, oh, God," someone was saying brokenly.

Celia was aware of startled voices rising and falling around her, she was aware of terrible pain and weakness, but most of all she was aware of Lord Sherlay kneeling beside her, staring down at her, his eyes full of horror and grief. "Armin . . ." she mouthed.

"Oh, God, Celia . . . why . . ." he groaned.

"Love you . . . always have . . . so glad . . . did not hurt you . . ." She could say no more because everything was growing very dark and, regretfully she realized she must be dying.

"Fortunately, she's a healthy young woman—and the fever from the wound was slight, my Lord. That, I believe, is because we did not bleed her."

It was, Celia, thought, a very odd remark for an angel to be making, nor was the voice in which it was uttered very angelic. Though she had never speculated as to how such voices must sound, it seemed to her that rather than being gruff and grating, they would be pontifical like that of the minister in St. George's Church—he who had performed the marriage ceremony and might have presided over her funeral—though actually, she did not feel dead. However, she had had no experience in being dead—but from the way various friends described the specters that were supposed to appear on the turrets of their ancestral castles or in various corridors, they had always seemed vague and misty, whereas she still felt solid. It was, however, very dark. She could see nothing—then she could and that, she realized, was because she had opened her eyes. Did ghosts need to open their eyes? She closed them again because the room was bright with sunlight, then she opened them a second time, quickly, because she had glimpsed a tall familiar form, standing with another smaller form. Then she could not restrain a sob, for memory had come rushing back and, with it, her vision of Lord Sherlay and Vandrington and what had happened . . . then her husband was kneeling by her bed, and astonishingly, he was much thinner—in fact, his face was actually haggard.

"Celia . . ." he said tentatively.

"I . . . I do not . . . believe I am dead . . . after all."

He laughed shakily. "No, my love, you are not dead."

She was extremely startled by his form of address—

because she knew he did not love her. Yet his fingers were
in her hair, brushing it back gently—certainly she must be
dreaming. She expected he would vanish directly—as
dreams always did. It occurred to her that she had been
having many dreams of late, but she could remember none
of them. "Am I dreaming . . .?" she asked the dream by her
side.

"No . . . you are awake at last and you are on the mend,
but I suggest you do not talk now, my dearest. You are yet
weak and need to sleep."

"But I am not sleepy and I want to know . . ." But even
as she spoke, she knew that she was drowsy, very drowsy,
yet marvelously content because she could tell Armin was
no longer angry with her and he had called her "love" and
"dearest."

Armin was in the hall, talking with the doctor, who had
just rebandaged her shoulder. He had pronounced himself
well satisfied with her progress, but Celia, hearing his dron-
ing voice through the open door, wished he would not wax
so prosy. She wanted Armin to return. She had been told
that it was the afternoon following the moment when she
had first opened her eyes. She marveled over that. It had
seemed no more than a minute but actually it had been a
full day! She did feel stronger but she had trouble reassuring
her husband as to her relative freedom from pain, he having
suffered a similar shoulder wound in Portugal. She flushed,
remembering his light dismissal of that hurt—causing her
to believe him a coward. She had been so wrong about
him—in so many ways. She smiled then, remembering and
treasuring the conversation interrupted by the doctor's arrival.

"When I saw him with you . . . I wanted to slay him with
my bare hands," he had told her, his face pale with remembered fury.

"I thought you hated me," she had said.

"I thought I did, too—until I saw you struggling against him. Then I knew the truth . . . and when you threw yourself in front of me and were so hurt." His voice had broken. "God, it was the height of folly for you to do such a thing."

"But he would have killed you," she had explained.

"As it was, you might have died, and our child with you."

Amazingly, incredibly, the doctor had discovered that she was breeding. She could hardly believe it—she had told him so, asking if he could not be mistaken. The doctor had countered with some incisive questions as to her health before the accident. Had she suffered moments of queasiness and had there been other physical manifestations? Since her answers had all been in the affirmative, she could no longer doubt her condition—and in spite of the wound, her baby was safe. It was a strange, wonderful notion and Armin had seemed very happy about it, too, but there was still much to discuss, much to understand. No one had mentioned Vandrington nor asked why he had come to play cards with her in her husband's absence. Nor did she know why Armin had returned from the theater so unexpectedly, and now that she was truly awake, she was eager to tell him things based on what Vandrington had told her. For the first time, she realized what a shock it must have been for Armin to arrive at Bella's house and discover what seemed to be her duplicity. She could imagine Vandrington's insinuating voice as he had mouthed the half-truths which had hurt them both so terribly. She pounded her fist on the bed. "He has to know!" she cried.

"Who has to know, my dearest?"

"Oh," she gasped as she saw Armin coming back across the chamber. "I did not realize I was speaking out loud."

"To whom would you impart this knowledge . . . love?" he demanded.

"To you," she told him. She stretched out her hand and he took it between both of his, caressing it. "You must know everything, everything I was too proud and too angry and too hurt to tell you. Will you listen?"

"Perhaps you should wait until you are stronger," he said.

"No, now," she insisted. "Listen, do."

Pulling a chair close to the bed, he sat down. "Very well, but if I see that you are tired, I shall stop you immediately." Having delivered himself of that statement, he was very quiet as she spoke. She had started bravely, but as she explained her lack of knowledge concerning her birth, concerning the situation in Bella's household, concerning Mrs. Moulton, it seemed to her the height of stupidity that she had not guessed the truth. Indeed, as she faltered to her conclusion, she feared he would never believe in her innocence and might even imagine as did Lady Emily that, in addition to her other stratagems, she had snared a senile Lord Chadbourne. "I . . . I was very unhappy after my illness and L-Lord Chadbourne was kind . . . and he knew everything that had happened . . . so when he asked for my hand . . . I acquiesed . . . I . . . did not really care . . . what happened," she finished lamely.

"Your illness." He frowned. "Were you ill?"

She flushed. She had not meant to mention that. She had not wanted to play upon his sympathies. "I was ill for a time . . . afterward . . ." she mumbled, making it worse by inadvertently touching the lock of white hair, "but it was of no consequence."

"Oh, God, oh, Celia . . ." His hand was in her hair stroking that parched lock.

Looking up into his face, she saw that tears were streaming down his cheeks. "Don't . . ." she said softly. "It's all right now, Armin, my darling. We're together."

"But the years . . . the long, lost years . . ." he mourned.

"Think of the years ahead of us," she begged. "There's no one can take those away from us."

"No," he agreed. "No one in the world, my beautiful."

* * *

The walled gardens of Briarton Abbey were famous. The late Lady Angelica Sherlay had, with the help of an inspired gardener named Tweed, developed the Angelica Rose, a pale pink blossom which grew in a special plot surrounded by red, white, and golden roses—all collaborating to fill the heated August air with their heady perfume. Near the rose garden was a covered bench by a pool filled with fat Japanese goldfish. Seated on the bench were Lady Alys and her hostess, Lady Sherlay. Though both were in the thinnest of muslin gowns, they were assiduously fanning themselves.

"Oh, it is warm. I should follow the example of your Cousin Laura and go inside—but it is so very pretty here. I expect that old sundial over there dates back to the time of Abbot John?"

"And before," Celia said.

"This is such a beautiful old place. I adore Abbeys."

"I, too."

"You are looking wonderfully contented."

"I am . . . utterly, and now that dear Cousin Laura is out of earshot, I can say that I owe it all to you."

"Oh, no." Lady Alys shook her head. "I did but tell him . . ."

"You told Armin that Vandrington was coming to play cards with me and that I was deathly afraid of him. Angry as Armin was with me, he still decided to investigate. If he had not . . ." Celia shuddered.

"But he did!" Lady Alys shook her head. "That miscreant. Imagine drawing a gun on a man who was supposedly his best friend! I never liked him—that morbid way he had of dressing . . . but, he'll not wear gray in Botany Bay." Lady Alys giggled. "I vow I did not mean to speak in verse—though Sir Charles did, occasionally."

"I remember," Celia said dryly.

"But I never dreamed that Armin would have the Bow

Street Runners ferret him out, much less appear before the magistrates to press charges of attempted murder. However, I am delighted at the turn of events. He'll not wreak any harm on you from the wilds of New South Wales.

"No." Celia smiled. "I should never have had an easy moment while he remained free—not for my sake so much as for Armin's. I am sure he would have tried to do him harm." She glanced at her husband, who stood talking with Lord Rolf. His auburn hair gleamed in the sunlight and was reproduced in a somewhat lighter hue upon the head of his little son, whom he had lifted from his carriage, much to the annoyance of Rose, who had taken over the duties of Nurse since her marriage to the Torleigh's one-time footman, now installed as an apprentice butler in the Abbey.

"I can hardly believe that you both intend to remain in the country," Lady Alys remarked. "Will you never come back to town?"

"Oh, I imagine we'll visit it from time to time—but I know we'll not stay long. Armin prefers it here—and so do I."

"I am glad that you do not regret the loss of the Chadbourne Luck . . ."

"Celia, dear," Lord Sherlay called, "come here a moment."

Beckoning to Lady Alys, she moved toward him, and on reaching his side, she put both arms around his neck and kissed him. He looked surprised but gratified. "What might that be for?" he asked.

Linking her arm through his, Celia turned to Lady Alys. "Would you say that I'd lost it?" she demanded.

"No, you certainly have not." Lady Alys smiled.

"Lost what?" Lord Sherlay demanded.

"Luck, my dearest love," his wife replied.